CHAINS OF FATE

ANNA M WARD

ZTOPIAN BOOK GROUP

CHAINS OF FATE

Rachel A. Davis

∾

This is a second edition under a new pen name. If you read the original by Rachel A. Davis the only difference is a chapter misprint for some editions of the original print book and minor grammar fixes.

Chains of Fate

Edited by: Amy T. Schubert

A Ztopian Book Group Book

Published by Ztopian book group

www.ztopianbookgroup.com

ISBN (trade paperback)

Ztopian Book Group books may be purchased for educational use. For information on bulk purchases, please contact Ztopian Book Group at ww.ztopianbookgroup.com/contact.

Second Edition: April 2026

∾

1

4 MONTHS AGO...

∾

Jessie stared at the front doors to her school. The building just stood there. Unaffected by all that happened. Even the people surrounding her were unchanged. Laughing and running through these halls. Maybe it was still too early for her to try to come back to school. It'd only been two weeks since the accident. Sarah's death was still too strong in her mind. She refused to believe that just a few months ago the two of them had been like everyone else. Celebrating Sarah getting her driver's license. It felt like they had all the freedom in the world.

But something had changed. They no longer laughed together. That piece of plastic in her wallet had flipped some kind of switch in Sarah. She started going out to more and more wild parties. Then the experimenting with alcohol began a month ago. The obsession to hang around with the rich wild crowd. Leaving Jessie behind. No longer were they the inseparable odd couple. It was questionable if they had even been in the same universe towards the end.

It wasn't their duo falling apart that had shocked her - Jessie had always expected that. People always seemed to leave her behind. But she never thought it'd come so suddenly. All because Sarah had turned sixteen a few months before her. And even with Sarah's new personality, the accident still seemed to come out of nowhere. Even through all the stories of wild parties, she had still preached to her about the dangers of drinking and driving. Sarah had even called her house one night for a ride. So when Sarah's parents had called her she was sure it was some kind of twisted prank. But, Sarah's car had collided head on with a drunk driver at cursed corner.

Jessie's parents hadn't said a word as they rushed her to the hospital. One of the few times her parents supported her, and Jessie had been grateful. The injuries were a death sentence. In less than twelve hours from the phone call Jessie had to say goodbye, the only one who had been at Sarah's side the entire time. Willing Sarah not to leave her behind. It felt like Jessie was dying with her.

Focus. If she didn't start moving she'd be staring at the gates all day. Like some kind of psychopath. Her breath caught in her throat. A darkness seemed to be pressing down on Jessie. More memories tried to overwhelm her. Deep breaths. She had to do this. For Sarah. Just one foot in front of the other. Ignore everything else. Their goal had been to graduate from high school together. At the same high school they started out. For Jessie that would be an accomplishment. Her whole life had been one move after another. It was her parents' response to her seeing the ghosts. Her parents did not believe in the ghosts, or anything supernatural. They assumed she was crazy most of the time. Shipping her off here and there to get help.

Speaking of the ghosts and her crazy parents, the gods had been kind to Jessie the past two weeks. She had not seen any sign of Sarah's ghost. That would have been enough to send her over the edge. Giving her mother the ammo she needed to ship her off, permanently. It was no secret that her mother saw her as a failure. Something that needed to be purged. Her mother's distaste for her was probably just as much to blame for her breakdowns as the ghosts. Very few of them were actually dangerous. They just acted out, wanting attention, like a toddler.

It was why Sarah had been so important to her. For the first time in a long time, interacting with the ghosts had no longer been stressful. Bringing her back to her childhood when she had been more curious than stressed by their presence. She was almost ten before she had her first glimpse at a ghost. It had acted like a guide or an imaginary friend.

How so much has changed. When the ghosts first appeared to her they were fuzzier. And silent, usually. It often felt like she was listening to the whirs of a radio station not quite in tune. Since they often helped her, mostly finding lost toys or keys, they didn't seem scary. When she was ten most people thought it was cute, even if she was a bit old to be having imaginary friends. As she became older she learned that it was less cute and more worrisome. By middle school Jessie kept the ghosts a complete secret to anyone, especially her parents.

Jessie shivered as she reached the door to the school. It was hard now to tell the difference between the ghosts and the living. The ghosts could be a bit transparent when they wanted to be. But most of the time they were quite solid. Blending in with the living. Their voices just as loud as a living person's. So much energy wasted on trying to pick out the dead from the living. The worst was when the ghosts decided to manipulate their surroundings. Usually it felt like she was falling into another world. Losing herself in a place where the dead ruled.

Glass doors. Finally she had reached the entrance. It felt like she had run a marathon instead of shuffling the thirty feet to the door. As the warning bell sounded, the air grew heavier. The ghosts were here in force. Angry about something. But what? Jessie couldn't remember promising them anything, it never ended well. Maybe if she kept moving they'd go away, or at least stay at the entrance. She had been spotted by teachers so it wasn't like she could run. Her mother was just looking for an excuse to send her away. Running out of the school screaming at nothing would be all the evidence she needed.

She's halfway to her locker, at this pace she might only be five minutes late to class. She knew she should move faster. But the energy wasn't there. The room seemed to shrink. Turning black. The color seemed to bleed from the world. She was slipping into their world. The air was so thick she was struggling to breathe. She doubled over. Trying to catch her breath. If she was going to survive the day she had to pull herself together. If she couldn't even make it to class then graduation was out of the question. At least at a normal high school.

But it was becoming harder and harder to care. Her house of cards was falling fast. Jessie glanced down at the floor and shoved her hands deeper into her pockets. Forcing herself to ignore it. Them. Everything. Whispers started to swarm around her. Sucking her energy. The whispers seemed to be twisting into a snarl, coming for her. Wanting her. It was impossible to tell what was coming from the living and what was coming from the dead. Which wanted to bring harm to her the most. Everyone...everything glared at her. Wanting to destroy her.

Her breath caught in her throat. Stumbling around the corner. Tripping over nothing. Her locker came into view. Just a few more feet down the hallway. The world seemed to right itself. The air thinned out. Jessie wiped her hands on her jeans, trying to hide the sweat. She took a few deep breaths. First encounter survived. It reminded her how much she had come to depend on Sarah for everything.

She swiped at her face. This was not the place to cry. She'd had two weeks to cry it out. But it was hard. Sarah had been her source of light. Someone to ground her in reality. To stop her from self-destructing. And then when she needed her most Sarah hadn't been there.

Jessie shook her head. Forcing the darkness away. If she wanted to make the final stretch to her locker she had to focus on something positive. That had been Sarah's strength. The first, and probably the last, person who believed her and accepted her powers as normal. Not once questioning her sanity. She felt herself smiling thinking back on the huge amount of time Sarah had spent on the Internet searching for answers. Wanting her to have a normal life. Connecting her with others that had similar powers to her own. It felt like Sarah had wanted to prove to her that she wasn't a freak.

But no one seemed to see ghosts quite in the same way as she could. Many of the connections she made through Sarah had turned on her much like her own mother. Worried that she was dangerous or going to bring the end of the world. That had never slowed down Sarah, or scared her off. That was the amazing part about Sarah. She just brushed it off and moved on to the next idea. It was why Jessie had let herself get attached to someone again. And now so many of her defense barriers seemed to be faulty. Still affected by Sarah's warmth.

Finally she was at her locker. Well almost. Jessie pushed through the crowd trying to reach her locker. Why were so many people still in the hallway? She could have sworn she heard the tardy bell ring while she struggled to move. Was there someone popular near her locker? Popular enough that people would be late to class. She couldn't remember anyone. Then again if she was at her locker everyone seemed to take off, not wanting her reputation to damage them. No matter how far she ran the rumors about her abilities always caught up to her.

But something was definitely going on by her locker. It felt like half the school was here now whispering and pointing. Maybe she had imagined the bells going off. After all these years maybe she was as crazy as her mother claimed. She stumbled through the crowd into an open space. Glancing up, she noticed her locker. Something was carved all over it. But she couldn't focus on it. Something else was causing her to freeze in place. Jessie tried to get herself to move, to say something. But she was captivated by the scratching noise coming from the inside of her locker. The noise that no one else seemed to notice. Deep breaths. She tried to keep her hand from shaking as she reached for the lock. It needed to be open.

A slight hesitation. Her world seemed to shrink. Darkness closed in on her. The whispers from the other kids drifted away, until it was silent. The only thing still in focus was her locker. Calling to her. Somewhere in another world a teacher was yelling something about clearing the hallway. All she cared about was her locker and what was inside. Her heartbeat echoed in her ears. It almost drowned out the scratching noise. Almost.

She stretched out her hand. Willing herself to open the stupid door and get it over with. Standing here trapped between two realities wasn't an option. That had been her whole life. Trapped and afraid. If she couldn't do this she might as well admit defeat and check herself in. One last deep breath. She spun the code in. Jessie flung the door open. Blood came pouring out. It shimmered and danced in the light. A loud scream pierced her ears. Her own? Someone touched her shoulder. The darkness engulfed her.

2

THE CITY IS BUZZING BELOW AT THE RETURN OF THE SUMMER residents. Zen stumbles up the stairs to his apartment, the headache growing with each step. The mind wipes are getting harder and harder to bounce back from, his memories fleeting. He needs to get his thoughts straightened out before the interview. Things never end well when the mind starts to fall apart. He wishes he could remember what happens in the interviews. He can't have much time left before they find him and force the issue. His cover may finally be blown.

He made it to the fourth floor. Zen falls into the door as he searches for the keys. Please don't let them be left behind. He can't seem to focus. Change falls to the ground as he digs through his pockets. It seems like hours pass by the time he finds the key. He rams it into the lock. Half jiggling half turning the key. The door flies open. Zen tumbles onto the floor.

The little black book. He needs to find it. How did he forget about the book? Without the book there's no way he'll pass the test. He just wishes he could remember where it is or what is written in it. Time is running out. This is not going well.

Zen shuffles through the trash, knocking over stacks of paper. In the middle of the papers on the floor he spots it. The tiny black book. He snatches it off the floor, trying to remember how long it's been since his escape from the compound. As he goes to open the book a small bracelet falls out. The thick black band seems familiar. Along with the small charm that hangs from the middle of the bracelet. He'll figure out what it means later. He slides it in his pocket as a stack of papers falls over. After this meeting he really needs to clean up the apartment, his shift here almost done. He thinks. Flipping through the pages of the book is clips of his life from the last five years, but more importantly there's a list of instructions. The whole reason he fled Var, returning to the apartment. Without this he is sure to fail the test.

A shrill ring reverberates off the walls. Zen looks around for the source. A green phone bounces on the screen, crap. He approaches the laptop carefully, trying to figure out where to place the book. Which pages to keep visible. He sits it to the right of the laptop out of view of the camera. He tries to puff up before answering the call.

He blinks, staring at the screen not sure what he is looking at. Why is there a white capital R floating on his screen. Did he not get to the computer in time to answer the call? The red light glows next to his camera.

"Hello? Someone there?"

"Took you long enough to answer. The elders aren't happy about your little jail break you know."

"Who is this?" The letter disappears, replaced by a black haired girl.

"It's Raven. The letter didn't give it away? To think you're this out of it and you're running around. You know you have pass the knowledge test after a mind wipe. Now let's get your test over with Mr. Runaway."

"Why you? Can't the elders do it?"

"Of course not. You know they spend most of their time in the board room. I'm not happy about this either. As third best agent I have better ways to use my time. Now tell me what a Psyren is."

Zen can't remember. He lays his head in his heads, trying to steal a glance at his book.

"They're magic users. Once part of a secret coven who worshiped the creatures they are humans cursed by the creatures. They can control memories, manipulate emotions, create seals and open the gate into the Abyss."

"Good. Now sit up! You don't take anything seriously. An Astro?"

"Also part of the secret coven. They are able to communicate with the creature, come and go from the Abyss as they wish, and in rare cases they can see the future. The more powerful ones are unaffected by the Psyren's magic."

"See was that so hard? Congratulations on being the second person in our ranks to reach seventeen without losing their sanity with all mind wipes. Try not to run off next time."

The screen goes black. Zen lets out a sigh of relief. Somehow he's able to get through the quick test unnoticed. He thought he was caught for a moment when she yelled at him. Now he just needs to piece the rest of his memory back together before anyone else calls. If anyone realizes he's hacking it Var will lock him away or whatever they did to the Death Walkers who were no longer useful. The other problem is his other side is trying to rise up and take over. It's taking advantage of his mind being so clouded. He's not ready to become a creature. Zen remembers enough to know what happens when a Death Walker loses their human side to the creature blood.

He slides onto the couch with the book flipping through it. This may be the last chance to study and he needs to rebuild his memories before the next test happens. There's no way there will not be more fallout from his breakout of the Var base. It's unheard of to leave before they deem you fit for the field. Even someone with his bloodline can't get away with some things.

3

____

Fox cruises down the highway. He reminds himself to slow down before hitting the town limits. Small town cops are always looking for someone to bust. And then there is the mountain weather to deal with. His truck had come off the line a long time ago. Fortunately it hasn't started really snowing up in the mountains yet. It is close though. September has just begun and he's seen plenty of signs of winter's approach along the way.

The timing of the plan couldn't be more perfect. It's the combination of the coming winter weather and Tyr's medical advancements. Since Tyr's branching off from Var centuries ago they have finally made their own major breakthrough. Behind the veil of their pharmaceutical company they are a few months away from perfecting chips that allow the Psyren to control any creature from the Abyss. Although with his natural ability to control the creatures he will not get to be one of the Psyren testing out the chips on the field. They want to test his ability against their chip.

The near perfection of the chip is why he pitched his plan on how to take over now. It's much easier to get the creatures to go along with Tyr's plan if they have no choice in the matter. There would only be five Psyren needed around the globe for his plan to work. Carefully knocking out the seals surrounding the Abyss, combining the two worlds. Since it is a slow moving plan, Fox initially believed the board would overlook it. They always act like they want to swoop in and destroy all the seals in a few hours. Whoosh, bang and a new world order. But that never works for them, and somehow Fox has managed to convince the old geezers at Tyr to go with his more realistic plan to take over the human world.

With the boards' acceptance of his plan Fox's rise to the top is now complete. It's hard to believe just two months ago he was a nobody when pitching his plan to take over. And he has the older generation inside of Tyr to thank for it. All that listening about the history of the creatures and the Abyss has paid off. Fox blends Tyr's desire to open the gates between Earth and the Abyss with his own desire to destroy the humans and Var.

The credibility with the elders inside Tyr comes with doing what no one else does. Fox actually reads the reports coming in with the various informants. He's learned about a lone Astro with a connection to Var, yet they never brought this Astro into the organization. Or are even monitoring the Astro. For Var to do something so careless, it seems too good to be true. It's an easy decision to pitch a plan to the elders giving them what they wanted while also getting his revenge on Var through this Astro. There isn't a better calling card to the enemy.

All he had to do is convince the board to go along with him, and they have. To all of it. Now less than a month after approval he is on the road. On his way to open the first gate into the Abyss. Soon he can get revenge for his sister. And the new world order can begin. Let the filthy humans be devoured by the creatures from the Abyss. Maybe he can swing by his old town and try to break the seal around the gate. Let the creatures destroy it. If some creatures destroy the town a second time those religious nuts might not rebuild a third time. The thought of blood-filled streets causes him to let out a twisted laugh. Almost like a snarl.

However that will be far in the future. It will take several open gates before the creatures are able to leave the Abyss. As of right now there isn't one open gate. This mountain town, Solace, would be ground zero. The only kink left in Fox's plan is Var. Usually Var just sticks to the shadows throwing money at the media from their hedge funds to keep any knowledge of the Abyss secret. Their defensive nature grows stronger as the number of Death Walkers keeps shrinking. But Fox knows that messing with the seals will force Var to go on the offensive, causing them to toss their money around in other places. While most of their Death Walker agents are useless, with bloodlines more human than creature, there is one exception. A 'pure' Death Walker. Zen Kros, a fifty-fifty split of human and creature. How the Kros family managed to do that with access to the Abyss cut off is a mystery for the ages. It's been hard for Fox to get Zen where he needs him for the plan to work. Zen has fallen in the ranks since an accident when he was much younger. The accident that involved the lone Astro that no one is remembering to watch. If all goes well both this Astro and Zen will end up in Solace around the same time. Tyr already sent a Psyren, the best at emotional manipulation, to go convince the Astro to come to Solace. Fox is banking on the Astro's powers to once again attract the creatures necessary to finish destroying the seal. Even if Zen somehow survives, he'll be broken and changed.

A glance at the GPS tells him he is getting close to Solace. Fox tries to focus on the present. He could revel in his brilliance later. The fog is getting pretty thick for this time of night, and he needs to focus on the road if he is to not fly by his destination. He still doesn't trust the accuracy of the GPS, but it beats a map.

It is the witching hour. Midnight. The perfect time to begin a new project. A small sign peeks through the fog. The truck flies through Solace. What a small town. A few seconds and he's through the main street. If he blinked he would have missed the town. The people of Solace have no idea what is getting ready to hit them. None of the remaining families in the town have any bloodlines linked to the Astros or the Psyren. They won't be able to see any of the creatures. At least not the weak ones that will come out of the gate first. It is part of the beauty of the whole plan. With hundreds of gates to be opened, Fox doesn't want anyone around that could sound an alarm. He wants a head start before Var gives chase.

The GPS screen begins to flicker. The little icon spinning out of control. It is enough to make him dizzy. The truck coasts to a stop on the side of the road. He slams his fist on top of the box. Nothing. A sigh escapes his lips. He is going to have to do this the old fashioned way. At least the cemetery is supposed to be on the same road as Solace. If he goes slowly enough hopefully he will see something from the road. With the fog thickening, it is hard to know for sure.

Fox pulls back onto the road, looking for any signs of the cemetery. This is not the time to lose his cool. He does not need to attract attention before he attacks the seal. It's too early in the plan to have to play cat and mouse with Var. And even though the board have given his plan the green light they would be just as quick to replace him if Fox catches too much attention. The only thing they care about is recreating the Heinzer event. Successfully this time.

He squints out the windshield. Willing any sign of the cemetery to emerge through the fog. His excitement is wearing off. The longer he is out here, the chance to run into one of Var's Death Walkers increases. Somewhere between town and the cemetery is one of Var's outposts. A big fight isn't something he wants, especially so close to the humans. It was a stunt like that which caused his sister's death and the reason he turned to Tyr. They allow him to express his hatred of all humans. The humans are more twisted than the demons they fear.

A rusted piece of metal appears on his right. He slams his foot on the brake. The truck lurches to a stop. It looks like a fence. A tiny red imp runs into the fog. One of the creatures coming back from a prank. He wonders what it is doing to choose that form. Usually when the creatures pull their pranks they prefer to take on a more human form.

With the creatures running around Fox decides to walk the rest of the way. He can't risk flying right past his destination trying to spot the entrance. He has already spent too much time up in the mountains. Pulling his jacket closed, he glances down at his wrist. A slight adjustment to keep the bandage in place. The tattoo artist had tried to go through his arm. Somehow the triangle actually came out looking normal. As he slides out of the car he slips his sunglasses on. With this kind of weather there is still a chance he could run in to someone, like a lone cop. He is in no mood to get in a fight tonight over his red eyes.

As he steps out of the car he is greeted by the fresh crisp air. And then there's the sweet silence. Fox runs his fingers through his hair, wiping extra gel on his pants. He could get used to the cool mountain air, but he has to move. The gravel crunches under his boots. Approaching the twisted metal he finds a fence, or what is left of it anyway. And on the other side are tombstones. He has found the cemetery. If he remembers the layout correctly, the seal is somewhere in the back of this place.

Fox doesn't feel like finding the entrance. He launches himself over the remains of the fence. Once on the other side he takes small steps. Listening for any movement other than his own. A few crickets chirp in the distance, the only other living things in the area. Maybe the fog isn't so bad after all. It's become a natural layer between him and the human world. Such an ugly world. Dirty. Soon that will all change.

As he strolls towards the back of the cemetery, the green glow of the seal comes into view. The old gate screeching open. It seems like the humans built a cemetery onto the old Death Walker cemetery. Irony at its finest. He trips over a half buried tombstone. Focus. His goal is so close. Fox walks through the Death Walker cemetery reaching the other gate. Why this cemetery is broken into three parts is a mystery. The seal is completely in view. The four statues, representing the four directions, surround the seal like silent guardians.

His mind wanders as he looks up trying to find the highest part of the seal. A perfectly shaped dome sitting between four statutes. Rumors had it that there is a fifth statute near the center of the seal near the gate, but only an Astro would be able to see it. It's amazing to think that the seals have survived centuries unchanged. A single Psyren centuries ago created the first seal, cutting off the Abyss from Earth. It's hard to believe something like the seals around each gate into the Abyss is what ended the Heinzer event. It almost seems a shame to even try to break the seal. Thousands of gates around the world sealed all at once by one person. And not one has failed. It is amazing.

Though the Astros are truly the lucky ones. Sure he can see the creatures, but he can't communicate with them. And the Astros can freely walk in and out of the Abyss. Yet so few of them took advantage of this gift. Most choose to help Var keep the humans safe and the worlds separated. Sacrificing themselves to protect the seals. Fox can't understand why they squander their gift, siding with Var. He would love to see inside the Abyss without fear of being trapped.

Fox sighs. It's time to get started. To crack the seal, but not destroy it. He has to have control. This is the main difference between his plan and those before him. He doesn't want to break the seal completely. If time has proven anything, it is that it takes a great amount of power to break a seal. More than one Psyren could possess. Even one as powerful as him. No he is just going to crack it, and make it easier for the weaker creatures to escape. To explore Solace, and find the Astro he has coming to town. Maybe cause a few more pranks than usual. The creatures' desire to consume the Astro would cause more of them to come through the gate, eventually breaking the seal. The magical power from the lower level creatures of the Abyss should be enough to shatter the seal. No reason not to use that power to his advantage.

Fox lifts his hand towards the seal. Closing his eyes. He holds his breath. Listening. The sound of glass breaking. He opens his eyes, coming out of the trance. A tear has formed down the seal. But it is still standing. Pulsing as it tries to mend itself. He waits for a moment to make sure it can't completely repair itself. It's still pulsing but a two foot tear remains, its rejuvenating power dried up. Fox checks one last time that it isn't fixing itself before he starts the jog back to his truck. Time for the games to begin.

4

Two months. That is how long Jessie has been stuck here, Wayport Home for 'Troubled Youth'. It seems to be some kind of recovery hospital. What for she still can't decide. She's seen everything from drug addiction to mental illness. A catch all kind of place. Before landing here she spent two months in Wayport Hospital. Drugged up and abandoned all because of some stupid ghost pulling a prank in her locker. At least here she is left alone most of the time, instead of being poked and prodded at the hospital. She's been allowed to wander freely for almost a month now.

Her daily walks are how she found this beautiful garden, tucked away from the rest of the center. She enjoys hiding among the multi-colored roses and some kind of purple flower that is in the back. There is even a bench being claimed by the roses. She keeps meaning to ask someone what the purple flower is. Maybe she could plant her own flowers when she is allowed to go home. Her own personal garden to relax in.

Jessie runs her hand along the flowers as she wanders toward the back. There is something relaxing about this place and the lack of ghosts. If only she could recreate the same atmosphere outside of this place. If she found a way this could be her last trip to one of these places. The normal life.

The bench comes into view. She plops onto it, looking up at the yellow roses that make a natural canopy. Her summer is already gone, her sixteenth birthday inching closer. It is still a mystery how much longer she will have to stay here. Both the doctors and the nurses avoid the question. Never a good sign. Though she isn't letting it bother her right now. Her parents toss her into a crazy house after every breakdown and she hasn't broken the record of six months yet. She'll start to panic if it nears the six month mark.

Still she is anxious to return to school, and is trying to rush her release. There is no way she is going to let the ghosts win. Her promise with Sarah is more important to her than ever. The pre-sixteen Sarah, her Sarah, had given up the life of a popular girl to be Jessie's strength. Pushing her to make what seemed like an impossible promise to graduate together. And Jessie knows that the longer she stays here the more likely it is that her parents will make her change schools. It makes her nervous. Especially since her parents have been avoiding her. Not visiting, and leaving the phone unanswered.

She sits up. Pushing the roses away from her face. In the distance she could hear one of the nurses calling for her. It isn't dark yet so what is going on? Another meeting to talk about her feelings? Thankfully this time she has fewer meetings with a shrink than her other visits, but the irregular schedule means it's easier to miss an appointment. This is the first time, and probably the last time, that bullying will save her. Everyone thinks the vandalizing of her locker caused her breakdown. And she is able to see why after seeing some of the pictures.

The writing carved into the outside of the locker had been things like 'die witch' and 'burn'. Even taking the time to paint it red. They had gone for the extra credit. There has always been talk of her being a witch and all the stereotypical responses to witches had been carved into the locker door. She's heard them too often to let such insults bother her. But she isn't going to tell doctors that. Inside had been the worst of it - the inside of the locker had red-stained razor blades and a noose. So all her screaming has been attributed to that wonderful prank. Avoiding any talk of ghosts. Which is fine by her.

Her parents are even playing along with the doctors' theories about stress and bullying. But she suspects they know the truth. Otherwise they would visit her more often than they have. Or at least call. But, like her, they want to get Jessie out of this place as soon as possible. Though it is with less than noble intentions. Months from now she knows her mother will still be griping about all the money she costs them because of 'her problem' with seeing the ghosts.

Jessie freezes near the garden's exit. What if this is Sarah's friend coming to visit her again? She couldn't handle another visit like the first. Jessie knows the other girl had meant well. Wanting to warn her about the school climate. But it is still hard to hear about it. That the whole school had conspiracy theories on how she had caused Sarah's death. Everything from how she is jealous of her friend's new popularity to being a crazy witch. They all end the same. She had cursed Sarah, which of course had caused the accident. The normal rumors that seem to follow accusations of being a witch. If she had the types of power people thought she had she'd have cursed herself a long time ago to get rid of her powers. Have that normal high school life Sarah had tried so hard to give her.

Well, no reason to put this off. No matter what is going on she doesn't need them to come in and drag her out. First, it'll make her look crazy. Second, she might lose her privilege to wander the garden freely. She forces herself to walk the last ten feet to the exit, holding her breath. Her tension level rising the closer she gets. Jessie stops as she exits the garden. A strange new doctor is standing with the nurse. He isn't sporting the same blue jacket as the rest of the doctors either. What is an outsider doing here? She doesn't like it.

Near a table are her parents. They haven't been here for most of a month. They are also hanging around this strange new doctor. Everyone is swarming around this guy like he is some kind of rock star. Hanging on his every word. Fawning over him. Jessie keeps waiting for the fan girl screams. She has a bad feeling about this handsome stranger. The same sinking feeling she had at her locker is returning. He's human and not human. Like her and not like her. He looks up and meets her gaze. She fights the urge to scream when he flashes her a smile. Her instincts are telling her to run. To go hide in the roses. Out of his sight. This is the first time she ever feared a human more than a ghost, only making it harder to walk towards him.

The logical side of her feels silly for being so afraid of a doctor. They have never done anything to harm her before. And if he is like her there's no reason to afraid, the worst that ever happened was few insults. She forces herself to walk towards everyone. Not letting her instincts and imagination win over. Running away wouldn't get her out of here. Besides, doctors call in outside experts all the time. A fresh perspective is what they call it. Overworked is what Jessie calls it.

As she nears the small table, he extends his hand. Flashing another smile. Reluctantly Jessie shakes his hand. A wave of calm sweeps over her. The fear that struck her before melts away. Being afraid of a doctor, maybe she is becoming crazy. She glances over at the cluttered table. It is full of pictures that he's laid out. Some stones sit on top of them to keep them from blowing off in the wind. Her parents are checking them out, eliminating some and enjoying the others.

"What's going on? What's with all the pictures?"

Her mother turns to face her. "The doctors don't think there's a reason for you to stay. But you can't go back to Wayport. This doctor is here to help us find a new city for you."

"Why can't I go back to Wayport? I'm able to face the bullies now."

"It's not safe for you. Things have only gotten worse while you've been away. Besides look at these pictures. Doesn't this place look so cute?"

Jessie comes closer. Looking at some of the pictures the doctor brought. She is drawn to a photo of a small house surrounded by woods. It feels like home. She flips it over to see the location. Some town called Solace. The doctor peers over her shoulder, going into a long speech about the place. Not interested.

The feeling of unease returns as he talks and moves closer to her parents. It feels like this situation should bother her more than it does. How often do doctors act like real estate agents? She steals a glance at her parents. They seemed calm and relaxed about the whole situation, for the first time in years. Maybe this isn't so weird after all. It isn't like she has ever had a normal life anyway. As the doctor drones on she picks up other photos of Solace. As he moves in-between her and her parents her interest for this new town begins to grow.

5

It's been almost a month since the mind wipe. Zen still can't remember much of his own past. He needs to start putting more than just tactical information inside his book. Like why in the world he is carrying around this old bracelet with the symbol of hades on it. Or his instant dislike of Raven. The second test was even worse than the first. By the end Zen wasn't even sure what he was yelling about.

Shortly after the test is finished he's informed that a seal has been disturbed. Since he is the closest to Solace he is lucky enough to be sent out here. At first he thought he would get to stay at the current outpost, but the elders refused. They want Zen closer to town so they sent him to an abandoned outpost less than a mile from Solace. He can tell it's been a long time since Var used this place. Zen leans on his old corvette deciding if he should go in. He fidgets with the bracelet on his wrist as he checks the house over. It looks like it is about to fall over. A relic to taunt the Death Walkers, his people, on how far they've fallen. So few of them left. Which is why he's ended up here holding a report that he can't remember how to read. Unfortunately that is another thing that didn't make it into the book. For now he will just report based on what he can see and hope it's enough to trick everyone back at Var.

With September ending and the snow already falling he hopes it will be a short wait until the Psyren arrives. A sports car on the snow-covered mountain roads is not going to end well. This crap always seems to happen in his patrol zone. Though with only five of them left on the continent it probably doesn't help his odds. And now he is stuck playing the waiting game. Instead of getting to chase down the person who attacked the seal. If it's one of Tyr's Psyren the chances are slim that they will give up after one seal. So he has petitioned the elders to let him chase after the culprit, relying on his ability as one of the best trackers. Plus there is the added bonus of it giving his memories more time to recover. Being one of the best trackers he thought he had a chance. But, no luck. His petition had fallen on deaf ears. The elders are sure that the person will come back and try to finish breaking the seal. They insist that a half broken seal wouldn't be their intention. But Zen isn't so sure. From what he can remember Tyr is always thorough. Having enough back up plans to to make a prepper look ill prepared. If that seal is meant to be broken it would have been broken. There is something they are missing. And that makes him nervous.

Zen reaches the porch, as he looks it over he doesn't need a level to see how uneven it is. Getting crushed by an old rotten porch isn't on his to do list. He stretches his foot onto the first step. Tapping the old wood. Still standing. He decides to tiptoe across the porch, just in case. Once at the door he hears a low rumble, like something is snapping. He flings the door open. Stumbling inside as the porch comes down. Is this house really safe to stay in?

It has been abandoned a lot longer ago than he thought, the dust gagging him as he enters. On the outside it looks like a small farm house, but that is deceiving. Zen guesses that at least a dozen different people could have lived here at the same time. Inside along the hallway some of the old family portraits still hang on the walls. Old mixed with new. It is unnerving having all these smiling faces looking at him. He is surprised that this old outposts has not been scrubbed like all the others. Var doesn't like the Death Walkers finding pieces of their past, before the constant mind wipes and fear building began. When they lived like the humans, side by side. Having a family and a home.

But those days came to a swift end after the Razen event thirty years ago. The last time Tyr tries to recreate the success of the Heinzer event. Between the two events the Death Walkers took a huge hit. There isn't even a hundred Death Walkers left within Var Corp. Maybe another fifty still survive outside of Var. Those traitors at Tyr have made sure of the Death Walkers downfall, directly and indirectly. It's why Zen hates the magic users. It has always been easy for the Psyren to break mentally, and they don't care what has to be destroyed to get their way. Zen has only met a few Psyren that aren't a twisted mess. Trying to bring attention to the two organizations. It would be nice to not have to clean up after the Psyren all the time. Zen feels more like a babysitter than a proud warrior for the human realm.

The further he goes into the house the more it resembles the outside. Wallpaper sliding off the wall, and dust painting the floor boards. Zen runs his hand down the wall. Wanting to see what the house looked like before. In the living room is a similarly sad story. Everything from the lamps to the chairs are covered in sheets. Like someone had planned on coming back. The once-white sheets have become gray under all the dust. It is hard to imagine what this place had been like when it was a functioning outpost.

Off in a corner is smaller furniture, like a child's corner. He lifts up one of sheets. Handmade dolls, wooden cup and ball and several other old wooden toys. Some are cracking and falling apart from age. This is probably before the Heinzer event even. Back then it would have been unusual to walk away from an outpost. He wonders what happened here. Why did the children leave all their toys behind? Why hasn't this place been sterilized like all the other houses? He drops the sheet back onto the pile of toys, wiping his hands on his pants. The situation is unsettling.

Zen returns to the hallway. Going further toward the back of the house. The kitchen is clear of any relics. All that remains are a few lone sheets on the chairs. The table lost its sheet. He sweeps his arm across the table trying to knock most of the dust off. On top of the table he drops his bag. It seems like a good place to start. He slides his laptop out of his bag, trying to ignore the forgotten relics inside the house.

A life he is never meant to have. At birth the Death Walkers are separated from their parents, to build their dependence on Var. Their family is the organization. Not that it matters to him. His mother had tried to kill him before Var found him anyway, terrified of his other side. The identity of a Death Walker is whatever they are told, they are more like well-trained pets than people anymore. They are always erasing one identity for the next. It's the only reason they keep the Psyren around. But its price is high. No matter how many times he goes through the book the only thing he can remember is his first name. It is the last connection he has to his human side. To him it is important. Giving him the strength to not lose himself to the creature blood running through his veins.

6

The door slides shut behind him. Fox's daily meetings with the old geezers is over. He felt his anger rising with each passing minute he is forced to listen to their droning. As he walks toward the gym to cool down he wonders what the meetings would have been like if things had gone badly. It's been almost two months since he was last on the road. Something about travel delays for one of the other continents, so he is stuck at base listening to the old geezers' paranoid rambling.

As Fox approaches the building he hears the crunching of the punching bags. He glances out a window, shocked. Usually after the sun sets the place clears out. He hopes that it's just some of the older agents getting in some practice. The idea of dealing with the mouthy newbies just makes his mood worse. He pushes the door ajar peering in. It's the newbies. Fox sighs and tries to walk across the building to the locker room without catching their attention. The way they're all bunched together shouting and banging the equipment they are showing off. Trying to establish a pecking order.

"Hey bootlicker." Fox freezes in the middle of the room. He spins around to face them ready for a fight. The brunette from the middle starts waddling his way. He wonders how such a slob got to be the ring leader for this bunch of pests.

"Show some respect to your superiors."

"Drop the formalities, Fox. You're the same age as us. We're just curious how you got on the field before turning eighteen. What did you use to black mail the board?"

"Like I'm telling you shit. Get out of my face." Fox shoves the guy out of the way, his tension level rising.

"Must have been emotional plea then. Did you give them details about your sister's death? A poor me speech?"

Fox snaps. He spins around and charges the guy. Latching onto his shirt Fox rams him into the wall. Weights come crashing off the walls. Fox begins pounding on his face. Intent on teaching him a lesson, killing him. Something yanks Fox of his prey. He tries to locate the disruption as he is shoved against the wall. The grey uniform of security team starts to come into focus. He can feel their breath on his neck as the security officer leans in.

"Get out of my sight and maybe I won't tell the board about this little incident."

The officer lets go. Fox glares at officer's back debating whether to take a swing at him. He needs to leave and cool down. Before a bigger group forms, he slides out through the emergency exit a few feet away and jogs across the field to the dorms. Thankfully no one is out at this hour. Halfway to the dorm his hands begin to shake as adrenaline runs off.

Fox reaches the dorms and flings the door open. The hallway is deserted just like the outside. He slams the door shut, sliding down the wall. Blood splatters along his arm. Going inside the gym had been a horrible idea. The young recruits are always mouthing off. Their jealously runs wild and he shouldn't have expected to be left alone. But now they would remember their place. Fox wishes he could have gotten a hold of the whole group instead of just that one brat.

He stares down the hallway, soaking in the silence. It almost seems a shame to walk down the corridor ruining the silence. Fox has forgotten how little use this bunker gets anymore. The recruits all stay off base now. Everyone in the inner workings of Tyr has a place here but few use it, preferring apartments or hotels. He should have done the same. But it is convenient. Especially with the all the meetings he has to have with the board hashing out the final details. Making sure everything is going as planned in Solace.

A blood trail is following him down the hallway. Fox sighs and decides to clean it tomorrow. If security really does hold up to their end of the deal he doesn't need this evidence left behind for the board to hear about. He stops outside of his room. Across the hall from his room sits the bathroom. Calling to him. Fox walks in. Running water over his hands. The blood slides off as easily as it went on. He pulls a handful of paper towels from the wall dispenser. It feels like he is in training all over again. All the fighting and isolation. It has been part of his life since childhood. Even Wynne, his baby sister, had lectured him about the fighting. Until the humans killed her.

Fox returns to the empty hallway. For once he hates the silence. At his room he swings the door open. If everything goes well it is the last time he will be here. His relationship with Tyr would be over. Both parties getting what they want. With the new order controlling everything the secrecy will be unnecessary. He yawns, exhausted. He flops onto the bed. Moonlight drifts into the room from the small window. All this debriefing and lectures are exhausting. More so than the new recruits. The old geezers are more paranoid than he thought. Sure there is the possibility of something going wrong. He'd be surprised if something doesn't. Bringing down hundreds of gates around the world isn't an easy task. They aren't gods. And everything hinges on seven Psyren across the globe, one per continent.

But the risks don't matter. This time Tyr will succeed in recreating the Heinzer event, releasing the creatures into the human world. Soon, seals across the globe will be destroyed. Opening the gates into the Abyss wide open. Part of the reason Fox is so sure of the plan working is the timing. Like all things the seals have begun to weaken with time. One person's dominating power is finite. The first time, Tyr had been impatient. The last attempt at combining the two worlds again, the Razen event, had been an utter disaster. The only seals that were damaged then were accidents. Some even reported seeing the woman leaving the Abyss to repair the seals.

The archives deep in the bunker are useful, if one knows where to look. He's learned that after the Heinzer scare, one woman carrying the creature blood had sealed the Abyss from the inside. Creating all the green glowing seals that everyone sees today. If you believe the eye witness stories, she is a rare person possessing both Astro and Psyren blood. Her powers as a Psyren are true at least. She has made it almost impossible to open any seal into the Abyss. Let alone multiple seals across the globe. But something has happened over the last couple centuries. Even more so since the Razen event. Her powers have weakened. Most likely she has finally been killed. After all, the creatures couldn't be very happy to have been betrayed by one of their own.

Speaking of which, it would be interesting to see how Zen reacts when backed into a corner. Part of him wishes he could stay in Solace to watch the show. When Zen is faced with the choice between the town and the girl which would he choose? She has already been injured once due to Zen's carelessness. Him choosing the many over the one. Would that resolve apply a second time? Var's rules state that a Death Walker's resolve is absolute. It's the main reason Zen has fallen so far in the rankings. Waffling isn't tolerated. They insist on blind faith and loyalty that could only be challenged by a dog.

Fox never really understood why the Death Walkers chose to work with Var. It is obvious they are afraid of the creature blood that runs through their veins. It is why they are kept on such a short leash. Why else would they value the humans over anyone else? Var always choose the many humans over one of them. In some cases even choosing one human over a group of Psyren. It is ironic that it is the Death Walkers' humanity that is sacrificed to work with Var. For him it isn't such a big deal. He parted with his humanity the night his sister was murdered.

The lights snap off. Fox jumps. Is it already that late? Guess it is lights-out for the new recruits. Not that they actually stay here. He sighs. Laying back down, he listens to the banging of the old boiler pipes. Fox lets his mind wander to his next target. It is going to be a bit trickier. This time it is a bigger city. The one that the board had originally wanted him to hit first. Rayford, a city full of his people, at least while the festival is going on. He should feel worse about taking out his own people. But he feels nothing. If anything, he is full of excitement. All he has wanted since Wynne was killed, murdered, is to see the humans burn. Plunging the world into chaos. That night he had seen the creatures' power. Controlled it. He clenches his teeth, trying to forget and get some sleep.

7

Jessie shifts her bag around as she climbs off the train, fidgeting with the strap, as she looks around for a taxi. Her new home in Solace is supposed to be pretty close to Anchor. Which is good since Anchor is the last stop for the train. She's done enough traveling to last her a lifetime. The mountains seem so much bigger up close. She wonders if Solace is in the mountains. After living in the south for so long the idea of this cold weather isn't appealing. October has just started and already she can see her breath.

She looks around. A few taxies idle near the bus stop. Jessie grabs her suitcase, wheeling it towards the taxies. Picking out the least creepy driver. This is the part of the journey she isn't looking forward to. Why couldn't all of this happen once she was sixteen and could drive herself? It's less than two months out. Just once she wishes life would give her a small break.

Lights start to flip off. She dashes towards the taxies. No way is she getting stuck here overnight. They start driving away as she approaches. She taps on the window of one of the remaining taxis. Peering in. Time seems to stop as the window slides down.

"What do you want?"

"I need a ride to Solace. Sir."

"We don't go up the mountain. Try one of the guys on the street over there."

"Thank you."

Jessie gathers up her stuff and walks towards the street he pointed at. She waits for the buses to fly by. The calm she had getting off the train is disappearing with each passing moment. Why does she have to deal with transportation? Her parents should be here. At least wait to abandon her until she is sixteen and able to drive. She knows they dislike her episodes, especially her mother, but they always move with her. But this time her mother said they aren't coming. It isn't 'fair' for their life to be disrupted. She wonders how her parents are able to support two houses. They must be getting paid better than she thought. In that case, ignore the doctor and let her stay in Wayport. It is less stressful than this nonsense. They hadn't even taken her to the train station in Wayport or said their goodbyes.

Jessie notices an empty taxi driving by and tries to wave it down. The cab driver pulls over. She runs up to the passenger side hoping that he is one of the taxis that would go to Solace. The window slides down. She ignores the moldy smell coming from the inside.

"Excuse me, do you go to Solace?"

"Depends how far in to town you need to go. Some dirt roads up there have washed out. Never got fixed."

"Here's the address." Jessie passes the address to the young driver, hoping she is able to even get to this house.

"Should be fine. As long as the road back has been maintained. What kind of road goes to your house?"

"I'm not sure. My parents didn't want me to miss school during the move so I came first."

The man shrugs. "I'll try it. Climb in."

Jessie slides into the backseat of the taxi. This whole situation is making her more uneasy with each passing minute. She squeezes an imaginary stress ball trying to stay calm. The reality of the whole situation is finally setting in. Her anger is turning into depression and anxiety. If something goes wrong she has no parents and no guardian looking out for her. Everyone has tossed her away.

The taxi darts off zipping in and out of lanes. Cars blare their horns. It is much scarier when a stranger is behind the wheel. Jessie tries to stare out the window and ignore the erratic driving. She is stressed enough already. Looking back on the whole situation that landed her here, it is kind of odd. What kind of doctor picks out which town - hell even which house - his patients should move to? Maybe she should ask to stop at a hardware store. A couple extra locks on the house might not be a bad idea. She does not want a late night visit from some half-crazed doctor. She is keeping her visitors strictly to the dead, thank you. At least the ghosts have never been able to harm her physically.

As the taxi gets close to the edge of town it stops moving. She peeks through the windshield to notice that traffic stopped. Red and blue lights blur past the taxi. There must be some kind of accident ahead. All she needs. Another delay to starting over. She just wants to crash on her bed, and be in her new home already. The taxi crawls forward. The police clear the road of debris and gawkers. It is hard to tell if the gawkers or the accident is the cause of the traffic jam. Jessie glances away, not wanting to take chances on seeing any ghosts from the accident. No reason to risk ruining her luck now. It's been an odd sense of calm not seeing any ghosts the past couple weeks. On one hand she loves it but the other part of her worries about not seeing any ghosts. Seeing them is a reminder that she is still in her reality. That the ghosts haven't sucked her into their world.

Jessie catches sight of a fuzzy outline the size of a child on the other side of the street. It is staring towards the wreck. Her stomach turns. She watches the girl walk towards the wreck. Ignoring the living world as she walks through the cars. As she passes near the taxi something seems off. It is like the girl couldn't sense her. And Jessie isn't getting the usual vibe from the child. Why isn't she totally in focus? That is also something new. She forces herself to look away and stare at the floorboards. That is safe. Something about seeing the fuzzy ghost is more unsettling than seeing no ghosts at all. Like her powers are shifting. Changing. Reacting to something. She forces herself to focus on something else. This line of thinking is bound to drive her insane.

Snow starts to dust the ground about halfway up the mountain. So Solace is pretty far up after all. It's making sense why most taxis won't come up here. This trip started twenty minutes ago and is showing no signs of getting close. This far up she is going to have to go buy winter clothes sooner rather than later. Her winter clothes from Arkansas are not going to go far up here.

The road narrows revealing a steep drop off. Jessie prays that no other cars come from the other direction. She isn't sure there's enough road left for this to still be a two-lane road and she really doesn't want to find out. The taxi lurches to the right onto a winding side road. It slides back and forth along the road for a few feet, narrowly missing the rock walls on either side. Jessie relaxes as the ride smoothes out, finding the road. She wonders who carved out the road into the mountain. It seems like it's not natural since it is smooth and big enough to fit a semi. But like the main road, this one is narrow as well. It's like the roads were never adjusted for modern cars.

Jessie leans towards the window wanting to catch sight of Solace. She's curious to see if it really is as small a town as her doctor made it out to be. The road ends turning into a small driveway. That means Solace is further up the mountain. Great. Unable to drive and not in a town. Hopefully Solace isn't much further up the mountain. She starts digging through her bag looking for her runaway wallet. It always seems to make its way to the bottom and under something. She pulls it out and passes the fee to the taxi driver. Before she can slide out of the back he passes her a card.

"No transportation up here. If you need ride back into Anchor just call the office there."

"Thanks."

She climbs out of the taxi taking it all in. It feels like something straight out of a picture book. The small meadow the house sits in didn't show in the picture. She wonders if there are trails to walk in the woods. A nice hike through nature could really help her stress levels. For the first time Jessie feels like this move might not be so bad after all. She rubs the key to the house as she approaches the door. Unsure of what will be there, if anything, when the door opens. As far as she knows her parents never came out here and she hadn't been home long enough to pack anything from the house. She remembers her uncle briefly asking her parents about it the first, and only, night she had been home. They had blown him off much the way she had been.

The taxi driver sits there waiting for her to enter the house. Jessie unlocks the door and takes a deep breath. She flings the door open.

Boxes are all over the house forming neat stacks towards the ceiling. Some of the piles are taller than her. Now a bigger question forms of who has moved all this in? Is it someone from her family or a moving company who's been given an extra key? She pulls her phone out her pocket. She leaves her finger on the emergency button just in case. Plus there had been the odd doctor. She should have gotten the extra locks before coming out here. It is eerie being alone in the middle of nowhere.

First stop is the kitchen off to her left where she is able to drop her bags. The kitchen seems unpacked or at least isn't full of boxes. Just to make sure, Jessie opens a few cabinets to find neatly stacked dishes. On the fridge is a note from her uncle. At least someone cares. She reads the note as she checks out the rest of the tiny house. Apparently her uncle is the one to thank for a furnished house. At the back of the house are a bathroom and her bedroom. A sun room is attached off a back door. Since there isn't a second floor it seems like her parents have no intention of ever moving up here with her. What nice parents she has.

She finds another piece of paper in her bedroom. This one seems to be a map and instructions on how to get to town. Solace sits three miles further up the mountain. Somewhere there is a shed that holds a new bike that her uncle bought. He promises to come visit her in the next month or so for her birthday. At least one family member still cares for her. Jessie flops onto her new bed exhausted. She dozes off as she is studying her uncle's hand drawn map to Solace.

8

ZEN SHOVES THE RAKE DEEP INTO THE GROUND. HOW HAS HE been reduced to yard work? Is this really the only thing he could do all morning? He needs to get out of this place before he goes crazy. There are still two more weeks, at least, before a Psyren is able to get here. His lack of social skills is killing his choice in jobs. He isn't even allowed to talk to anyone down in Solace. Maybe working on his social skills wouldn't be such a bad thing. He hates people but this is getting ridiculous. Zen should be out chasing down the person who attacked the seal, not becoming a maintenance man to an old abandoned outpost.

Somehow this is more mind numbing than his usual outpost setting. He wonders if it is the isolation. Instead of being able to go in to town he is stuck with two options: work on this old house or sit in the graveyard staring at the seal. And staring at the seal isn't really an option since he's most likely get noticed in such a small town. A couple times, late at night, he's driven through Solace to check on the town without detection. Once the seal is repaired he plans on getting out of here. Immediately. At this point he doesn't even care where he goes as long as it is hundreds of miles away from this mountain and Solace. No more late night trips to the graveyard and, more importantly, no more damn housework. This is not his type of place. After this, he is going to put more effort to work back up the ranks.

He no longer even cares if he gets to go after the Psyren who attacked the seal. Picking up the trail after a month has passed would be near impossible. The weird part is that Zen hasn't heard of any other seals being attacked. There are whispers on the dark-net that it is an outsider. A debate is raging if it had been a fluke or a new group wanting to compete with Tyr. He hopes it's someone inside Tyr. The idea of a second group trying to merge the two worlds is terrifying. Either way, it means that this attack isn't random. Eventually other seals are going to be attacked. But who would want to open the gates but not agree with Tyr's philosophy? Is it insanity or ignorance? Sure, the creatures from the first level are harmless but if a lower level creature escapes it would be disastrous. He remembers reading the reports from the Heinzer event. One gargoyle like creature from the third level wiped out an entire town in two hours. Knocking over any buildings that didn't burn to the ground. He wishes he had copied some of the images into his book. The death toll from that one city has never been agreed upon.

Focus. It does no good speculating what could happen. Zen wanders to the front of the house staring out at the remains of the deck. A distraction is needed. His problem is what to do. There is always the daily drive by the cemetery to check on the seal. The skies are clear enough, he wouldn't need to stay long. He's already used up his bi-weekly trips to Anchor for supplies. Going into Solace isn't really an option since his trying to avoid being noticed. The snow makes it hard to even go on a cruise of the mountain. He really needs to get another old beater to use. One that is better for this kind of weather.

It's starting to snow, dusting the ground in white. Zen lets out a soft sigh. The roads shouldn't be too bad yet. Not that he cares what the roads are like; he needs to get away from the house. He tosses his jacket on as he walks out the door. The sky is starting to turn dark. This is going to need to be a quick trip if he doesn't want to walk back. The door on the corvette squeals open. It is about time to oil the old doors again. Zen slides behind the wheel and cranks up the heat. As the snow melts off the windows, he takes a minute to check the mirrors. Once the windows are clear he slams the corvette into reverse and peels out of the driveway. The car slides back and forth as the tires try to get traction. Zen lets off the gas a bit as he slides onto the main road. Maybe the roads are in worse shape than he thought.

As he approaches the cemetery he sees that the green glow has shifted. Something is happening. The seal seems to be reacting to something or someone. But what has changed? He stares at the dash trying to coax the corvette to speed up. Less than a half-mile to go. He glances up to see a blurred shape standing in the road. He slams on his breaks. Zen braces for impact as he loses control of the corvette. It slides sideways to a stop. A young girl is standing in the road staring at him. It looks just like her. He tumbles out of the car wanting answers.

He looks back up the road where the child had been -- she's not there. What the hell? Zen stumbles back up the hill. There's no footprints or sign of a person. He looks around trying to stay calm. Who is that girl with silver hair? It could not have been her; by now she'd be fifteen. There is no way it is her. He walks back to the car willing his hands to stop shaking. He needs to get out of here and check on the seal. Something strange is happening here and he needs to figure out what.

Zen starts to whistle as he checks out the corvette. Somehow it seems like there isn't any damage from the crazy slide back down the hill. As he inspects the front of the car he notices the red handprints on his windshield. They all seem to shimmer. Has the seal broken? The green glow still shows over the hill. He jumps into the car trying to race up.

9

The sun is starting to set, signaling an end to her first full day in Solace. It is not as world shattering as Jessie thought. It isn't even that difficult. Everyone at the school seems to be understanding of her messed up situation. Somehow she feels at home in this small awkward town. The principal even let her have the day off to finish getting settled. At first she thought it was a bad idea, but taking an extra day before starting school had turned out to be a good, and painless, choice.

Now there are only a few boxes left in the living room waiting to be unpacked. It is hard to believe how much stuff her mom has managed to ship out. The kitchen is packed full. There have been a few times she wasn't sure she was going to get the cabinets shut. She may have more gadgets and plates than her mother. How much does one person need? It's insane. And then there are all the books and movies. She could run a library and movie rental store out of the house. Did her mom keep anything in the old two-story house? It feels like her entire life, and previous home, is crammed into this tiny house. Like her mother is purging the family home of all things that remind them of her. A bittersweet ending to her previous life.

Jessie stands up and stretches. She counts the remaining boxes trying to decide where to put the rest of the things. Another bookshelf or

35

maybe a storage cabinet is going to be needed. The stacks of boxes make the house seem smaller. But how is she going to get anything to the house? It is still another two months before she turns sixteen. Even then there is no guarantee she can get a car with this new family arrangement. It's never felt so inconvenient to not be able to drive before. Thankfully someone in the city somewhat patched the main road to her place. It is at least good enough she can get her new bike up the mountain, which is all she cares about.

Her first trip to the town diner was interesting. Talking to some of the people at the diner, it's clear that no one had lived in this house for a while. There is no form of public transportation up here, which is probably why her uncle bought her the bike. Thankfully they are going to find someone to come get her trash down at the house. Pulling that up the mountain would not have been fun. The other problem is the doctors. They all operate out of the hospital, which is fine, except it's outside Solace another mile up the mountain. That's quite the bike ride when she isn't really used to biking. If she gets sick she is in trouble. Is she really going to be able to survive a winter up here on her own? Being an adult isn't as fun as she envisioned it being.

Jessie searches around for her backpack. She needs to at least look at what classes she is going to start taking tomorrow. It looks like similar classes to what she took in Wayport. She just hopes her mother gets the last of the paperwork back to the school tomorrow. How did she forgot to finish the paperwork for her school transfer? Thankfully the principal is willing to let her take classes for a week while they wait for her mother to return the paperwork. The principal wants Jessie focusing on adjusting to the new school environment and not on the adult stuff. It seems surreal that the town is so small that the entire school district fits inside an old factory building. There's still enough space left over at the school that most of the town could probably move into it. The secretary even gave her a map of the school complete with which door to use so she doesn't have wander empty space inside the school. It is both cool and creepy to have such an odd school.

Jessie finds her backpack and drags it along the floor into her room. She half tosses it onto her bed, planning on doing the homework she was given. No reason to start slacking off before she even starts school. With everyone being so nice to her today she doesn't want to toss it back in their face by being a slacker. Besides, why give a reason for her parents, more importantly her mother, to show up whining? No way. She is not going prove her family right and become useless. She might not be able to keep her promise to Sarah about where she graduated but she can still graduate. Jessie flops on the bed pulling out all the books, stifling a yawn.

10

ZEN PULLS UP TO THE CEMETERY. SOMETHING IS WRONG. THE seal is pulsating and changing size. He has to get back there. As he slides out of the car he keeps checking for any creatures. He darts past the cemetery gate heading straight for the seal. He keeps glancing from side to side checking for any creatures. It's empty. So far it looks like the gate into the Abyss is holding, even if the seal is not.

The next section of the cemetery comes into view. He slows down to a light jog as he nears the old section where the Death Walkers are buried. Zen stops at the gate to the next part of the cemetery watching the seal, mentally marking how far out the seal is expanding. The last thing he needs right now is to get trapped behind the seal as it expands. The statues are lost inside the seal, but it doesn't seem to be reaching this part of the cemetery. He reaches for the latch on the gate. It screeches open loud enough to wake the dead.

Zen lowers himself to the ground expecting trouble from the noise. There is no way that something hasn't escaped with this kind of disturbance. But what is causing it? He stays low and crawls towards his right trying to reach the other side. The seal just stops short of the final section of the cemetery. Halfway there Zen spots a group of creatures leaning and falling over the tombstones near the gate into the last section. Some of them have escaped after all. They are whispering among themselves and pointing towards Solace. Great. He regrets complaining about needing more excitement. This is not what he had in mind when he said more excitement. At least they haven't spotted him yet, giving him the advantage.

Before getting any closer Zen stops needing to plan his next move. They're in his way if he wants to get to the seal without going in it. He could turn around now and call the elders but that would leave these creatures to go to Solace and find whatever is catching their attention. He hides behind a tombstone as the seal shifts and grows. He peers around the corner to see what the creatures are howling in excitement about. The green seal is shifting, becoming almost transparent.

His breath catches in his throat. The black metallic cage glitters in the light, taunting him. Zen shouldn't be able to see the cage surrounding the entrance into the Abyss. A couple creatures, still in their wisp form, dance around the bars to the cage. He's frozen in place as the seal continues to grow reaching its breaking point.

The creatures' laughter pulls him out of his trance. He peers over at them. The creatures are shedding their human appearance for something more impish. A weird mix of an imp and the gargoyle like appearance of the more powerful creatures. They're close to leaving. Zen needs to decide what to do and fast. He can't let them reach Solace and find whatever it is that drew them out of the Abyss. He is not going to fail a second time. But what could he do with the seal in this state? If he tries to knock them into the Abyss they can walk right back out and come after him. The other option is to break the rules and attack them but that brings another set of problems.

The sun is beginning to set. Zen uses the shadows to sneak along the tombstones to get behind the creatures. As he makes his way around he keeps a look out for any stragglers. So far it looks like all the escaped creatures are staying together. Staying on the tombstones of his people. He slides his gun out staring at it. He knows it's made of some material from the Abyss, designed to only harm creatures. But he can't remember how it works. Will it stop after hitting one of them or does it keep going? Zen has to risk using it. This is going to be less diplomatic but it's better than them reaching Solace. Besides, what could the elders really do to him that they haven't already?

As he takes aim, something hard slams into his head. Zen crumbles from the impact. He tries to keep his eyes open as the world spins. The creatures surround him, smiling. Another one holds a rock over him as the world goes dark.

~

Zen's head is pounding. He opens his eyes trying to focus and remember what is going on. But all he can see is green. Green? His thoughts snap back into focus as he tries to move. Somehow he's on the inside of the seal, and near the center. He tries to think what there is inside the seal to even tie him to. The only thing he can think of is the final statue for spirit, but if that is the case it meant the gate into the Abyss is less than ten feet to his back. Way too close for his comfort - he needs to get out of here.

Also where are the creatures that attacked him? Have they made it to Solace or did the seal fix itself and they got sucked back into the Abyss. If Zen is to get out of here, it is important to know which path the creatures took. His ability to get out of here depends on it. If he is trapped on this side of the seal there's no one to protect Solace.

What is holding him to this stone? Zen stops struggling and looks down to see what is holding him in place. His own chains stare back at him. This day is just getting better and better. He tries to get some footing and slide up the statue to escape. As he works on his escape, Zen notices a red fog creeping along the ground. What the --? It's coming from behind him, from the gate.

He starts to slide around the statue, wanting to see what is happening. If something is going to attack him from the Abyss he at least wants to see it first. It feels like hours by the time he's able to slide around, facing the entrance to the Abyss. The cage over the entrance to the Abyss is gone. Zen stares into the small orb trying to decide what he is looking at. A dark forest full of old gnarled trees look back at him. Is this the Abyss or another gate forming somewhere in this realm?

The fog keeps growing, rising, almost choking Zen. He hears the creatures returning behind him, shouting in glee. This couldn't possibly get worse. He starts fighting against the chains holding him to the old stone statue, ignoring the entrance to the Abyss. The noise behind him turns from happiness to fear. Zen looks up, wanting to see what is bothering the creatures. The trees no longer float in the strange orb. Now it is a bright yellow light and he swears the orb is growing. He leans back trying to put more space between him and the orb. If he gets sucked into the Abyss he's done for. He can't get back without an Astro pulling him out.

Zen holds his breath as the orb continues to grow, swallowing him in the light. It feels like his skin is on fire but it's too bright to see anything. He's lost. There's no way he is getting out of this. He starts to hear screaming from somewhere, a girl. Has someone from Solace gotten trapped here to? Before he can call out, the orb shrinks. He blinks as the world returns to normal, like nothing happened. As the shock wears off he tries to get himself loose again. He starts to slide around the statue to make it easier to ignore the orb.

Some of the creatures come through the seal, walking towards him. One break - that's all he wants is one break. One of them reaches out for him with its clawed hand. Zen leans away from the creature. A bright light flashes past them. The chains fall off and he flies through the air. His breath is knocked out of him as he bounces off the ground.

11

THE WOODS THICKEN, CHOKING OFF ALL THE EXITS. THE trees seem to loom down over her. There is a small dirt path going north to south. The only place the trees haven't taken over. No other paths leading the way out. Strange. She is sure she had followed a path in but there doesn't seem to be one now. Jessie shakes her head back and forth trying to figure out where she is. There had been a path when she started, she is sure of it. Now it feels like the forest is leading her. Creating its own little maze. Telling her which way to go. She doesn't like it. Everything seems to be moving in slow motion. And where are her shoes? The ground is sharp and digging into her feet. She glances down and realizes the dirt is now sandy and filled with rocks and shells. It reminds her of the beach. But what is a path like that doing in the mountains? There can't be a beach around here.

She looks around trying to find the way out. As she follows the remaining path she watches dozens of ghosts appear out of nowhere with their heads down, walking southward. Like some type of death march. It seems like they are from several different eras and locations. She notices some of the ghosts in medieval armor and old tattered samurai armor like they are returning from a horrible battle. They are defeated and being forced to keep walking. A cross between a refugee and a slave. But what could a ghost possibly flee from? What could even control them?

Since the ghosts don't seem to be from the same time period, it couldn't be a loop from a natural disaster, or any kind of residual energy. So what's going on? Jessie's curiosity gets the better of her and she starts to follow the path northward. Maybe if Jessie goes the opposite direction she can figure out what they are moving away from. While she isn't a huge fan of the ghosts, she still doesn't like to see them tortured.

As she works her way through the crowd, she's more uncomfortable than normal. She doesn't like the odd vibe she is receiving from them. The ghosts seem to be multiplying. It feels like the path is looping and not letting her move forward. The ghosts are starting to notice her and wanting to talk to her. Each time she touches them she gets a glimpse of what it is they're running from. It's big, eclipsing the whole Earth in darkness. It's a crimson red fog, something from their world, but the center of the fog feels human. Anger and a desire for revenge. A demented offspring from both worlds.

Terror starts to build inside Jessie and she flees the ghosts. No more. She doesn't want to know about the strange creature or help the ghosts. She trips over a tree root and falls face down. The tree is warm, and she swears it's beating. She jumps up and tries to catch her breath. It feels like she's been running for hours not minutes. Glancing around she's back at where she started. That shouldn't be possible. Running in a straight line can't have put her back at the path.

The ghosts are continuing to multiply on the path. Whatever the thing is they had been showing her is beckoning them here. To this path. There has to be hundreds crammed onto the small path now. It is getting difficult to distinguish where one ghost ends and one begins. What kind of strength could that entity have? Trapping so many ghosts? A chill runs down her spine. She needs to get out of here.

Thousands of voices start to whisper around Jessie. The ghosts are finding their voices. Screaming for help. To not have to worship the entity. More and more voices join in becoming a single voice. The voices start to blend together in a horrible shout of pain. She covers her ears unable to make out what is being said. Not wanting to know. She struggles to breathe and stay calm.

She darts away from the path. Not caring where she ends up as long as it isn't here. Jessie needs to be somewhere away from the sound. The trees start to get thicker and twist together. A light mist turns into a thick fog. The darkness closes around her. She puts her hands out in front of her to keep from running face first into something. The darkness becomes so thick she can't see her hand any longer. For a moment she hesitates wondering if she should turn back. Jessie decides to keep moving. This is still better than the screams. It is impossible to see anything. She is forced to slow down to a snail's pace to keep from tripping over the trees. It feels like the voices are chasing her into the darkness. Are the ghosts leaving the path as well?

Jessie spots a patch of light through the darkness. She flees towards it not caring where it leads. Jessie trips over a rock and skids into the dirt. Crawling along the brush, she tries to reach the light. She ignores the scrapes and scratches that are forming. It seems like forever before she crawls into a clearing. The light is blinding after the darkness. The grass seems brighter. Almost like neon green. Her eyes wander towards the center of the meadow, where something is glittering in the light. A small pendant hangs from the boy's wrist. He appears to be around her age. She guesses around six feet tall. He has black hair and bright green eyes. He is just standing there like he's waiting for something. Unfazed by her noisy entrance.

The boy becomes surrounded by ghosts. As they close in around him she wonders if he can see them. It looks like a face off but it's hard to tell if he is staring at them or through them. Something shimmers. The boy trains a gun right at one of the ghosts. So he can see them. But how does he have a weapon made from the same material as the ghosts? He also seems to have a chain with shackles on each end. Whatever is going on, the outcome feels important. Not as important as what is happening past the darkness. But it is giving off similar vibes. Like this is the beginning. Or maybe the end. She watches the fight transfixed. Unable to look away. She knows she should keep running. But she doesn't want to. Can't. Her powers have glued her to this spot.

A ghost appears behind the boy. She panics. An irrational thought of the ghost harming him flashes through her mind. She tries to call out. Her voice is frozen. She can't move. Something is holding her feet. She glances down at dozens of red hands shooting from the ground. Wrapping around her ankles. They start pulling her into the ground.

Where the darkness is. To where the red thing is. The human destroyer. Jessie begins to scream and tries to break free. She watches as the boy gets overwhelmed and is lost in a mass of ghosts. It's over. The evil has won. She twists and turns trying to shake off the hands. Fighting the feeling of death coming over her. One of the hands shoots up to her neck. It wraps around her throat choking off her screams.

12

Zen tumbles onto his car. Everything hurt and his mind is a mess. That had not been what he had expected. And not just because he had walked into a trap for the first time in years. He can feel his creature side trying to take control. This couldn't be worse time for this to happen. Fighting to maintain control is draining the last of his energy.

Willing his memories to work, Zen tries to remember if his book mentioned something like this happening before. He can't remember. Heck, he can't remember anything even close to this has happened before. It's as if something inside the Abyss itself is reacting to something. But who and where? It's probably something close by. To find out what, he is going to need help from other Death Walkers.

As the car slides back down the mountain Zen fights to keep his eyes open. If this keeps up he is going to fall apart. Mentally and physically. Even with the creatures escaping and the entrance to the Abyss exploding, somehow the seal is still up. The same could not be said for other objects around the seal. The statue that held him is destroyed. He brings the part of it showing the spirit symbol as proof to show the elders.

Unfortunately, the creatures do not fare as well as he does. A half dozen or so have not survived the blast from the Abyss, and the others

46

he remembers seeing are gone. Hopefully they are in the Abyss and not wandering towards Solace. Zen knows he should check on Solace, make sure it isn't affected, but he's too tired. Besides, whatever the creatures are responding to will still be there in a few hours after he can get some rest.

The house comes into view. Zen never thought he would be happy to see this rundown building. He stumbles into the house wondering what to tell the elders. They are going to want answers, to know what exactly went wrong, and that isn't something he is sure of himself. Back in the house the whole thing seems surreal. Just a horrible nightmare. The piece of the statue reminds him that it really happened. Now is the time to figure out what the creatures want. What has changed over the last few weeks? His legs go weak. The old house outside of Solace. He has almost forgotten that it sold and is supposed to have a new family coming in. Could one of them be an Astro? It shouldn't be possible. Var keeps tabs on all Astro bloodlines.

He needs to file a report and to ask for help. If the elders at Var know what is going on it might be possible for them to send another Death Walker out. Or at least get a Psyren out here to repair this seal. He doesn't care about the schedule anymore. He needs a Psyren here now. The weaker creatures are already escaping at an alarming rate, if one of the more powerful creatures escapes it is game over. Solace has something the creatures desperately want and they are willing to destroy themselves to get it. It's that very desperation that frightens Zen. He knows the stories well of what happens when the creatures are able to steal the powers of the humans.

He makes it to the living room and melts into the couch. Zen pulls the laptop over, needing to type the report. To make contact with the elders. As he begins to type, something makes sharp raps on one of the windows. Zen freezes, listening to the sound. If the creatures are here to attack, it's all over. He can't even remember if he picked up his weapons before fleeing the cemetery. He slides the laptop off his lap, trying to decide where the noise is coming from.

Zen balances himself on the balls of his feet as he sneaks towards the back of the house following the noise. He pauses every few feet making sure the noise is still getting louder. It sounds like it is coming from the sun room. Maybe it's just a tree hitting the window. He flings the door open excepting to see another gang of creatures. Nothing is there.

Not willing to give up Zen peers out all the windows looking into the backyard. It's empty. No trees and no creatures. Is he finally losing it? His legs give out. The adrenaline from the last few hours is wearing off. He tries to stand and can't. Sitting on the floor he feels himself dozing off. He can't fall asleep - he needs to keep going. To figure out what is going on here. He sees the young girl, creature, that he ran over earlier in the day, peering into the room at him as he doses off.

13

Halfway through the day and Jessie still feels disjointed with reality. No matter what she does she can't shake the fear left behind from the nightmare. Their screams still echo in her head. She pushes her lunch away, her appetite gone. If she is going to return to the happy feelings from yesterday she needs to shake this dream. Already she has lost some of the vibe by her jumpiness all morning, freaking out at the smallest noise. Maybe she is finally going crazy like her mother always suspected.

Jessie watches some of her classmates walk by, pointing at her and whispering. Another reason to get herself under control, the rumors were starting thanks to her episode this morning. She still can't believe she had screamed when someone had tapped on her shoulder to pass papers forward. Ghosts can't attack people - pranks yes, attack no. Which is why there is no reason for her to be so uptight from a stupid nightmare. She doesn't want to be known as crazy or the witch girl here. All Jessie wants is a normal, peaceful life. She pulls her pants leg up wanting to check on her throbbing bruises. She still isn't sure how she managed to hurt herself during the nightmare. The bruises almost seem to look like a dozen tiny handprints, or maybe that's the fear talking. It makes more sense that she just kicked a bed post when trying to wake herself up. Things from her dreams couldn't actually harm her in real life.

She yawns, starting to feel her four am bike ride. Jessie had reached town by five exhausted. She stands up shuffling out of the lunchroom behind her classmates. Thankfully she hadn't appeared out of place arriving at the diner at such an early hour. As she had sat in the diner she noticed that most of the town ate their breakfast there. She had watched all the people going in and out. Seeing almost every resident.

One person she never saw was the boy from her dream. Jessie is sure it's someone she had seen lately. Friends appearing in dreams type of situation. Since there isn't that many people in Solace she thinks it should be easy to spot him. Reality is much different than her hopes. Since most of her class now found her slightly different she is afraid to ask any of them about the strange boy. She's on her own to piece this mystery back together. Proving to herself that she isn't crazy. For some reason Jessie just can't let it go. Something about the nightmare feels real, like when she slips into their world. If that is the case that means there is some truth to the red hands and the strange red creature. Maybe it is good that she hasn't found the mystery boy. The idea of any of that nightmare being true makes her anxiety level rise.

Jessie jumps as someone coughs in the distance, pulling her out of her thoughts. She snaps back into reality. Focus. She doesn't need another incident like this morning. The whispering of her classmates proves that they're starting to wonder about her. Think. What is a good way to wake herself up and stay alert? She notices a bathroom sign out of the corner of her eye. Perfect. She slides out of the line and into the bathroom. Splashing some water on her face should keep her awake for the afternoon classes.

She slides her bag off her shoulder and she kicks it under the sink. As she turns on the water Jessie casts a glance at her reflection in the mirror. Besides the giant bags under her eyes she notices a piece of silver hair peeking through. Real attractive. She makes a note to go buy a box brown hair dye after school. Finally the water is turning from brown to a more normal color. She makes a mental note to check on that later to see if it's actually safe to consume this water. She bends down and buries her face in the cold water. It feels soothing and her senses are returning to normal. It feels like she is finally able to shake off the last parts of the nightmare. There's a scratching noise above her, like tiny nails on a chalkboard. Curious Jessie stops splashing water on her face and glances up. She doesn't want a rat or something dropping on her head.

A reflection of a small child appears in the mirror, their face is covered by long black hair. Her head snaps around. Empty. No one's there. Reluctantly she looks back at the mirror, afraid of the truth. The child stands motionless in the mirror. Her mouth goes dry. Keeping an eye on the mirror, Jessie reaches for the handles, shutting off the water. She wants no surprises. Jessie tries to keep her eyes on the mirror as she bends under the sink to grab her bag. The child darts forward, slamming her hands on the mirror. Shimmering red handprints paint the mirror. A squeak escapes her lips. Jessie stumbles backwards and out the door wanting to get far away from the bathroom.

The hallway has changed during her short trip to the bathroom. A dark cloud seems to have settled in much like the tunnel vision she got back in Wayport. Dozens of ghosts have moved inside the school. Just take deep breaths and focus on reality, Jessie tells herself. While this isn't normal, there is no reason to let them torment her. If she ignores them, maybe they won't notice and bother her. Jessie closes her eyes as she tries to count to ten in her head. The important part is to stay in control. As she starts to walk away from the bathroom she hears a loud cackle behind her. She can't stop herself from running around the corner to her class.

14

He is halfway to Rayford. Somehow he had dodged any serious trouble for the fight at the gym. But it is making for a torturous drive. All the cornfields make it seem like he is not making any progress, or maybe that was the second day of straight driving talking. Fox notices himself dozing off and pulls into a gas station. He needs to grab himself something to drink and a short walk to keep himself awake. The last thing he needs right now is to fall asleep behind the wheel and crash the truck. Unfortunately a nap isn't an option at this point. He has to make it to Rayford tonight if he is going to keep to the schedule. He gets out of the car, hitting the door release for the gas tank. Since he's here he might as well fill up. If he tops off here he might even be able to make it to Rayford without having to stop again. Leaving him some time to nap at his motel before going out for surveillance. His muscles creak and groan as he climbs out of the old truck.

Glancing at the pumps Fox notices they're old. Really old. He isn't planning on using a credit card at the pump but these pumps don't give him the option anyway. Some of the pumps still have the old glass cylinders where he can see the amount of gas sitting in them. He's surprised that they are still allowed to use these things at a gas station. At least he's guessing they are allowed to use them since there is gas sitting in the pumps. He approaches the door to the gas station, looking around for any signs of life. Once he reaches the door he realizes all the lights are off. He tries the door anyway. Locked. Normally he would guess that it isn't a functioning gas station with such old pumps but he can see the gas. No big deal - he can make it to Rayford with the gas he has left. He isn't too far away from a small town, maybe the town will have a small grocery store. He really needs his caffeine fix.

Strolling back to the car, he hears a high-pitched scream. As Fox tries to figure out where it is coming from, he hears other voices joining in yelling. It is coming from behind the gas station. Fox knows he should leave it alone. If he gets in another fight the board won't hesitate to sideline him, but curiosity gets the best of him. He slides around the side of the building trying to stay out of sight. A group of large men have a small girl surrounded. Fox ignores the growing fog as he shuffles around trying to see in the center of the circle. The blonde hair and purple eyes are undeniable. Somehow his sister is here and is being attacked by a bunch of dirty humans. He charges into the group, knocking them out of the way. Wynne just stands at the center, not moving, blood running down her arm. He feels his anger rising as he stares at the word 'witch' carved into her arm. And are those burn marks? Not again, he won't let it all happen again. Fox lunges at the nearest person of the group.

Fox falls to the ground panting. As he stumbles back to his feet he looks around at the damage. Not one of the men is moving, but what happened to Wynne? He looks around trying to locate his little sister. Before he can call out for her reality sets in. There is no way that girl could be Wynne. The humans killed her over ten years ago. So who did he really see? Panic sets in as he shuffles away in the fog. He's already on thin ice with the board. If he is caught fighting with the humans in public, putting the whole plan at risk, he will be pulled off the assignment. And right now he could barely remember anything about the fight. His rage had been in complete control. Again.

An outline of a small child appears through the fog. The real victim from this whole thing. Fox runs through the fog, almost crashing into the wall. It still looks like his sister but this time he recognizes the transparent nature of the creature. After all these years he still walks right into one of their traps. His face turns red as he storms up to the creature masquerading as his sister.

"What do you want? Do you want to make me look like an idiot?"

The creature just stands there silently. Fox glares right back, refusing to let this thing win. He isn't some toy for them to play with, even if it did cause suffering to the humans. The creature points at the wall before vanishing. He grumbles and looks toward the side of the gas station wall. The creature had written in blood, the humans' blood, 'It's waiting in Rayford'. He shivers backing away.

Fox spins around and runs towards his old truck. He doesn't want to think about what is waiting in Rayford and what kind of trouble it will bring. As he sprints across the parking lot the fog lifts, revealing a totally different scene from his arrival. Gas no longer sits in the old pumps. He wills his hands to stop shaking as he tries to unlock the truck door. Whatever Tyr is stirring up isn't some weak creature from the first level. This kind of power is only something from the lower levels of the Abyss. And he isn't sure he wants to meet it. For a moment he wonders if he shouldn't have taken one of the jobs further from the front lines. No one truly knows what happens when the seals break and he wants to be around long enough to see the creatures take over.

The truck shudders as Fox slams the door shut, trying to catch his breath. He needs to pull it together. This is no way for someone like him to act. He ignores the blood on his clothes as he tries to start the old truck. Suddenly he wants to put as much distance as possible between him and this abandoned gas station. He checks his review mirror as he peels away. A red hand waves goodbye.

15

Jessie tosses the phone and watches it bounce off the table. What is the point of calling? She should have known her mom wouldn't tell her anything. Jessie kicks a nearby chair across the room. She had hoped her mother would have been willing to shed some light on her childhood, or mention if she remembers a boy with bright green eyes and black hair. But no, her mother told her to go through her yearbooks and to keep her 'crazy' in Solace. She was also reminded to not call unless it is an emergency. The catch her mother fails to mention is the lack of yearbooks, or any pictures for that matter, of her early childhood. There's nothing from before she is eight and she can't really remember anything before that either.

The phone call had turned into an hour-long torture-call as her mother laid out why it has been so hard to raise her. Tarnishing that perfect family image her mother had always envisioned. Jessie tried to imagine how hard it has been on her parents. They've always denied that she could see ghosts or anything supernatural. In their mind their daughter is psychotic. Disturbed. She has heard all kinds of labels growing up. To them her powers are imaginary. But does that really give them the right to abandon her in the ass-end of nowhere on a mountain? Apparently her mother thinks so. It is obvious she isn't welcome to call.

A sigh escapes Jessie's lips. She needs some kind of distraction to calm down. No reason to let her mother make this day even worse. Between the dream and the ghost in the bathroom at school she is enough of a nervous wreck already. She somehow managed to not run out on school, which is no small accomplishment. It still isn't clear to her what had happened. The ghosts just came out of nowhere and continued to hang around her until she got out of Solace. Like a floodgate suddenly opening. It reminds her of that awful nightmare from last night. What is changing here in Solace? All the cities she's lived in and the ghosts have never played peak-a-boo before. The whole presence of the ghosts here is different. Hungry. A chill runs down her spine.

The woods. Maybe Jessie could put this whole nightmare behind her if she can prove to herself that reality isn't like in her dream. That red hands really don't pop out of the ground and trees don't duplicate by themselves. It is worth a shot, better than sitting in the house going crazy. This type of activity had always worked with Sarah. Even if it is more intense here there is no reason why the same logic wouldn't work. And if she does find any of those things...well maybe she could prove to others she isn't crazy once and for all. Though she really doesn't want to find any of those things. Part of her would rather be crazy.

First things first: warm clothes. She heads to the closet, digging around for something warmer. No luck. The jacket from her uncle will have to be enough for now. It doesn't have a hood but that should be ok, there are a couple scarves she could use to protect her ears. Checking her pockets, she makes sure she has her phone, and that it's charged. Since she is near the back of the house anyway she decides to slip through the back door. For a moment she debates whether she should lock the door. Who would really come out here? Besides, this would make it a quick entrance if she does find trouble out there.

Once outside she wonders where she should enter the woods. She fights the feelings of being foolish for chasing after her nightmares. Part of Jessie feels crazy for even entertaining this trip. Pushing all other thoughts aside, she tries to remember where the whole thing started. It is most likely somewhere in the middle of the forest. She hopes that it is even this patch of woods. In the nightmare the only path she was able to see was the one the ghosts used. As if all the other paths had been wiped out by the forest. Or no other paths existed; it doesn't appear as if this patch of woods is well traveled.

Staring out at the forest, she finally decides to enter the woods near the east side. It seems like a good place to start. If she walks to the west, in theory, it should cross with the northward path she had taken in the dream. If it exists. A beach-like path in the mountain woods seems unlikely. But this is what the trip is for - regaining her sanity. As she wanders through the woods, she realizes how beautiful the mountains are. The leaves are still falling full of color. And they still make that satisfying crunch sound as she shuffles along.

After a few minutes into her hike Jessie finds the strange sandy path. Complete with the shells. She bends down, and runs her hands through the sand, making sure it is real. A branch snaps in the distance. Jessie jumps up and spins around. She's still alone. Must be a lone animal. She focuses back on the strange path. What is it for? There's no path going into the woods to lead to this point. Not even the remains of a path. And without any type of clearing there wouldn't be space to have another small house or building. Halfway up a mountain there's definitely not a beach, yet here is a path made of sand and seashells. The whole area feels wrong. She shouldn't have come out here.

Jessie tries to swallow. If she is going to see this to the end she has to go deeper. The meadow is somewhere away from the path. After finding the path there is no doubt in her mind that the meadow is in here somewhere. The problem now is remembering which way she had darted off the path in her nightmare. Think. She had darted up and to the right. She stops for a moment looking around to make sure she goes in the right direction. Does she really want to know? Her luck is going to run out. And there isn't really a reason to tempt fate.

Instead of leaving, she starts to veer towards the meadow. Jessie's feet have a mind of their own, leading her towards a destination. She is unable to stop moving forward, towards the meadow, like something there is drawing her in. Calling out to her. She fights the urge to scream. The trees seem to become thicker and thicker. Cutting her off from the safety of the real world. Soon all that's beneath her is tree roots and darkness. The ground is slippery. The darkness surrounds her. Suffocating.

She slips her phone out of her pocket, the backlight not beating back the darkness. She finds the flashlight app by memory. She needs to have some light. She needs to regain her composure. Nothing seems to be happening. Is it broken? She flips it around. Holding it up to her hand. The light is on but unable to penetrate the darkness. A sense of dread washes over her. If the meadow really is here, there's no way she is going to find it.

Her instincts tell her that she isn't meant to find the meadow today. A secret she isn't meant to crack. Her body starts to feel heavy, like a huge weight fell on her shoulders. Maybe it is all the stress she's dealt with the last twenty-four hours. Jessie starts to shuffle her feet, trying to turn around without tripping over anything. Once she is pretty sure she is facing west again she starts to walk forward. She is still holding the flashlight in front of her, not caring about how useless it is. Maybe she can get a better flashlight at the hardware store. Maybe one of those big floodlights could break this darkness.

It seems like an eternity before she feels the warmth of the sun once again. The sandy dirt path coming into view once again. She flips the flashlight off. It is easy to know where to go from here. To escape the woods. She sprints the last hundred feet back to the house. Jessie chides herself for letting a nightmare affect her so much. At this rate, she'll be a nervous wreck before the week ends. Back in another home. And this time her mother might not let her out. But she couldn't deny, things in her nightmare really do exist in the woods. A little too accurately for her taste. But dreams are still dreams. Ghosts don't haunt them. She glances back one last time at the woods. It is calling her.

Shaking her head, she goes inside. That is enough nonsense for one day. She slams the door behind her, throwing the deadbolt back in place. Closing that chapter for good. No more trips to the woods. Or chasing around her dream world in the real world.

But going down the hallway there is a weird sense of dread coming over her again. Part of Jessie knows there is some truth to the dreams. It feels like something she had gone through before. Something deep inside seems to be screaming that this isn't the first time her powers flexed their muscles. That this is how her life is really supposed to be. Shaking her to her very core.

Could Solace truly be awakening her lost childhood memories? Is there more to the ghosts than she thought? Impossible. Her powers are already beyond anyone Sarah could find. And it's not like she had been to Solace before. No déjà vu possible. She slides onto the couch closing her eyes, still wrapped up in her winter clothes. Her muscles ache and a headache is beginning to form from all the stress.

16

———

The old beater clangs to a stop. Run-down motels. Found in almost any city. Fox prefers them to a fancy place. In these rat-infested motels he is left alone. After what happened at the gas station he is more grateful than usual for these run-down motels. He feels dirty having been manipulated by such a weak creature from the Abyss. He'd controlled more powerful creatures than that. But he'd fallen for it completely. Not even hesitating. The more he thinks about it, the more he wonders if he has been manipulated by the manipulated. The plan to draw him in has been too elaborate for the first level creatures to have come up with. Sure, they are pranksters but they don't have any real powers to speak off. Something to look into later.

He glances around before heading into the office. No one around to notice his coming and going. He would have to throw his tattered and blood-stained clothes into one of the festival bonfires. Destroy any evidence. For now he would just have to keep it covered while he got a room key. As long as the person behind the desk doesn't notice he would be fine. Normally when the Death Walkers try to follow someone's tracks they tend to look at nicer places. All the young bloods in Tyr like to live it large on the company's dime. It's why Fox does the opposite and sticks to the more run-down places.

But those Death Walkers, they're thorough. Often checking every dumpster and every alley in a town looking for clues. Sticking out could be dangerous. He had almost been caught before even at a run-down motel like this. He slides his sunglasses on, as he climbs out of the car. Fox uses the side mirror to check out his face. No blood, thankfully. He runs his fingers through his hair, trying to tame it, while he approaches the motel office. As he reaches the door to the office he pulls the jacket tighter. Inside is an older man, fumbling with an old fashioned TV. Glasses thick enough to give him the bug-eye look. A good sign. Fox clears his throat to gain his attention. A book slides towards him. This place is stuck in the past.

"ID?"

"Here it is." Fox slides it across the counter. Praying his eyes are as bad as they look. That ID is one of worst fakes he's seen.

"201. In the corner away from office. Check-out's at eleven."

"Thank you."

Once outside he lets out a sigh of relief. That could have ended up much worse. And not just because of the blood on his clothes. Fox wonders if someone already has it out for his spot. Surely no one would make a fake ID that bad on purpose. The only thing they have gotten right is his gender. And his back-story is just as terrible. It sounds like something straight out of terrible B movie. Any other time he would be more worried about such an unrealistic work history. He hasn't even been alive for as many years as he has supposedly worked. But he doubts that at a huge festival questions about his work history will be coming up. Not exactly something people talk about while binge drinking. He makes a mental note to let the board know that the ID and history department are falling asleep on the job.

On his way to the room, he grabs his bags out of the car. He swings the room's door open. This is more run-down than he thought. There is even one of those vibrating beds in here. He almost wants to drop a quarter in just to see if it still works. The idea of parents having to explain this relic to their kids amuses him. He needs to focus. It takes Fox only a few seconds to change clothes. Stuffing the bloody ones into a bag. Later he'll need to find a bonfire to toss this in.

Crashing on the bed, he flips through the pamphlets about the festivities. It seems like the bulk of the occult festival starts tomorrow. October first. There is even a pamphlet in here for some religious nut jobs planning protests of the occult festival. Maybe he could pay them a visit. Nothing too dangerous of course. No reason to push his luck. Just enough to make them bleed a bit.

There's a parade tonight. Which means the alcohol is flowing freely. People's observation skills would be nonexistent by tomorrow. It would be a week-long event of partying and drinking. Most of the partying is planned to be in the town's center. Far from where he needs to be. Where most of the cops and any patrolling Death Walkers would be. The only way his fortune could be better is if there is an unplanned event or two by the cemetery. It would be an added bonus if there is someone with Astro blood at the cemetery and unaware of their powers. He would need bait to finish breaking the seal here too. He probably should have made plans to drag an Astro to every city where they attack a seal. Maybe next time.

Fox pulls out the map showing all the gates. An almost straight line all the way to the south. It is suspected that this circuit of seals Fox is destroying had been the front line of where that woman entered the gate into the Abyss. Sealing them off for centuries. The original circuit of the 'band of heroes'. Five people, all Death Walkers except for mystery woman, marching into the Abyss. More like the 'band of traitors'. Or suicidal idiots. No one can survive in the Abyss. The longest record is an Astro staying inside for two months before they died. The atmosphere is toxic.

It is ironic. Such an important string of gates to Var is also their weakest point. Once again playing a part in history. Just the way the board over at Tyr wants it, Fox could care less only wanting to bring down Death Walkers. If everything goes exactly as planned there will be about a dozen seals around the world wiped out within two months. Psyrens around the globe wreaking mass destruction. All at the same time. With only ten active Death Walkers around the world there is no way they could keep up. The final blow to a treacherous race. The thought of it all makes him shiver in excitement.

Fox sits up and slinks over to the desk. Pulling out the information on Rayford. The step-by-step instructions from the board. It's hard to concentrate. The events at the gas station are replaying in his head, making him on edge. Maybe a drink will help him relax, or at least take the edge off. He needs to focus on these plans if he hopes to not draw the old geezers' suspicion. Besides, there's no reason to worry about what happened. There had not been any cameras and with the fog no one would have seen him. As long as he doesn't tell someone of his mistake, no one will ever know it had been him at the gas station. Still he'd feel better once this is over and he could put more distance between him and the gas station. The goal is to be out of town in less than forty-eight hours. Soon Var will start sending Death Walkers to try to track him down. The goal is to stay one step ahead of them. They won't sit and watch forever. It isn't their nature. In more ways than one. The only thing still making Fox nervous is that Rayford isn't too far from a Var outpost. He knows this is the outpost that holds their equipment which monitors the seals' activity, making this one of the most dangerous towns on the circuit.

17

BACK AGAIN. THE CEMETERY IS NOT WHERE HE WANTS TO spend his afternoon, especially after earlier. Zen's grateful that he'd only been out for a few hours. Along with his body getting to recoup it somehow knocked cobwebs off his memory. It's less fragmented than it was before. Making it easier to think on his feet.

Before coming up here he had checked on Solace. The town had been fine. None the wiser that thousands of creatures are preparing to descend upon them. The more dangerous creatures seem to still be stuck in the cemetery. At least, that's what he hopes is happening. Only one way to find out. He pushes the gate open and walks toward the seal. Trying to look in every direction at once. If they aren't in the town they have to be here. But it seems quiet. Has he been fooled by their lack of activity in the town? This is one of the times he wishes he had better sight to see the creatures, or at least an Astro here to assist him.

The emptiness is unnerving. He feels his tension level rising. Even the old section where his people are buried is empty. Not even one of the weaker creatures is around to taunt him. Nothing around the seal. Hundreds of creatures just don't disappear. He has never seen them willingly go back into the Abyss either. This whole situation is bizarre. He wishes the Psyren were here and fixing the seal. Something is wrong here. It is possible the escape last night had been a fluke. Something caused by the tear in the seal. It seems to have gone back to its normal size. The green glow he's accustomed to has returned. Before the seals went into place, it isn't like anyone had tested them. And to his knowledge, this is the first successful attempt at destroying a seal partially. If this becomes a trend it is something they'd have to consider in the future.

Just to be sure, Zen walks around the seal. Looking for any changes. If it weren't for the lump on his head he'd question if he were hallucinating the whole thing. The place is so quiet. And so is the town. Nothing is here. Had this strange behavior from the creatures been part of Tyr's plan or an unintended consequence? And what had caused the creatures to come flying out? The more powerful creatures usually don't bother coming out of the Abyss unless there is an Astro nearby. Something to feed on. And there isn't one in Solace. He'd double-checked that before arriving.

He leans on the fence. Trying to put all the pieces together. Before coming out here he had been chewed out by the elders. Losing a fight wasn't something they took to well. They also want some definite answers to what happened. In their eyes, either the gate is open or it isn't. They are sure it couldn't happen both ways. And normally Zen would have agreed with them. But now he isn't so sure.

The elders now want visual confirmation if the gate is open. The problem is Zen can't actually see the gate. Not now that the seal has returned to normal. That is a gift reserved for the Astros. Which of course he isn't and there isn't an Astro coming. There is no way anyone with Astro blood will come near the seal now that it's going crazy. That would guarantee the gate being open. And if he goes into the Abyss the chances are good he'd end up trapped in the Abyss, unless the seal goes haywire like yesterday. But the elders aren't ones for calm logic right now. They'd expect a mailed letter from the inside. Death Walkers are expendable. Even when they are near extinction. He thinks they'd be relieved if the Death Walkers are wiped out.

Zen grumbles as he stares into the wreckage zone where the seal sits. Part of the fence is gone and pieces of the spirit statue still litter the ground. Somehow the other four statues are still standing. Not even a nick. The returned normalcy is unnerving. He needs to decide what to do and walk through the final gate to face the seal. He could jump into the seal and pray he doesn't get trapped in the Abyss. Assuming the gate opens up and lets him in. Or the seal could spit him out on the other side of the cemetery. It all depends on the condition the gate is in. And how strong the seal really is. Something he isn't sure of anymore. Last night as the battle raged on, he would have sworn the seal was all but destroyed. For him to be able to see the gate, the seal would have had to be at the breaking point. But now it appears as if nothing happened. Like a twisted dream. Part of him knows he has to find out what is happening, and not only to keep the elders happy. It is possible the unstable nature of the seal could have destroyed this entrance into the Abyss. A new entrance could be open somewhere without any type of gate or seal. Just an open portal. Putting more than just Solace at risk to be attacked by creatures. If something bad can happen it seems to happen in this town.

Zen stands up, choosing a second option to investigate the damage. It isn't ideal but it is better than being stuck in the Abyss. If that happens the town could be defenseless for a month before another agent could get here. He strolls up to the edge of the seal, careful to not actually touch it. He'll toss his chain in to see what happens and what it touches. If it comes out the other side of the seal than the gate's still closed. He prays to the gods that he doesn't hook anything too dangerous doing this. His muscles still ache. He checks the length, still enough energy left to get about twenty feet. Hopefully that is long enough to get something, and not something that just pulls him in.

He takes a deep breath, calming his nerves. Zen starts to swing the chain, taking careful aim. He squeezes his eyes shut as he lets go of the chain. It flies into the green aura cutting through the seal. A soft clang sounds as it makes contact with something. He walks around the seal. It is the gate. Ok, maybe closing his eyes isn't the best idea. He lines up with the middle of the seal once again. Taking aim. This time it disappears.

18

JESSIE DODGES A FEW SQUEALING KIDS ON HER WAY TO THE
locker room. They wave an apology as they disappear, she hopes they
make it in time. A sense of normalcy is returning to her. It's been a few
days since she had the second dream, waking up screaming. For that
Jessie was glad. It feels like her sanity is fleeing her with each dream. Her
powers have never reacted so strongly to anything before, as if the ghosts
are in her head, warning her about something. The red hands? The boy?
It is hard to tell. The ghosts that had appeared in the school had been a
lot less forceful with their thoughts, which made her stomach sink even
further. She had tried to pick up where Sarah had left off, researching
about her powers. Looking for similar experiences. As always, it had
been a whole lot of conspiracy theories and not anything useful. There
has to be at least one other person in history with powers like her. If
nothing else, someone in her family must have experienced something.
She's sure she read somewhere that this type of thing is passed down
through the bloodline. But Jessie knows she would get further talking to
a brick wall than asking her mom for help. She is not that desperate. Yet.
Maybe if the Internet couldn't turn up answers she would need to be
more old-fashioned in her approach, like checking out old history books
in the library.

Jessie shuffles into the locker room. She is trailing behind her classmates, exhausted from the fake friendliness. Besides, this way she can listen in on some of the elementary girls. There's something refreshing about their innocent laughter. It reminds her of a more peaceful time in her life. At first she was uneasy about sharing the gym with such a young group. Now she loves the chatter and laughter of the younger girls.

As she enters the locker room she shuffles to her dark corner. It is an appropriate place for her locker. In the back. Isolated from others. While trying to remember her locker combination she realizes that the room is empty. Even the younger girls who always seem to be late. Did she really fall that far behind the rest of her class? She tries to remember when she lost the sound of their chatter, but can't. She shrugs it off and unlocks her locker. A tardy here and there isn't a big deal.

A loud metallic bang echoes through the room. Jessie lets out a soft shriek. What is that? It sounds like half the lockers are coming down. It happens again. Flashbacks to her last high school play like an old record. She slinks down the rows of lockers, slowly approaching the sound. It could be a kid trapped in a locker. Or someone playing a joke. Not every sound has to be the end of the world. Taking a deep breath, Jessie peers around the corner. An open window. And a locker door whipping around in the breeze. A sigh of relief. She chides herself for being so pessimistic. This is what leads people to be crazy. She walks to the middle of the locker bay to shut the door. It's littered with reminders of the young girls who use the area. It doesn't look like anything actually makes it into the lockers. Jessie shuts the door.

As she turns around something creaks. Confused, she looks back. A shadow falls over her. Glancing over she notices the whole row of lockers is crashing down towards her. A scream catches in her throat as she scampers out of the way. Looking up, red hands disappear into the wall. Jessie is frozen in place for a few minutes. It's coming.

Jessie scrambles to her feet and dashes for the door. Once in the hallway she looks for the nearest exit. She is getting out of here and going home. She doesn't care what anyone thinks. It isn't safe. It is coming. The red fog. Memories of the red mass in her dream return, the hands. She shivers. Leaving everything behind she escapes from the building, tearing down the hallways. The doors fly open as she crashes through. Ignoring the cold she dashes for the bike rack, needing to get away. Her hands are shaking as she tries to unlock her bike. Someone is yelling at her. A teacher? An adult? She doesn't look up. Jumping onto her bike she flees the school, going down the mountain as dangerous speed. If the red hands are real then so is the boy. Jessie has to find him.

19

Unending darkness. Jessie checks to make sure all her body parts are there. No light seems to reach where she is. She crawls along the ground trying to find her way out. Or a light. This must be where she ended up when the red hands pulled her down. Soft tremors erupt over her body. Even though she knows this is another nightmare, it feels real. After a few moments of shuffling along she realizes that she is the only thing here. In the cold darkness. She can't sense anything else here. Wherever here is. Not even sound penetrates the darkness. It isn't safe to be here. She needs to find a way out of here. Up is not an option. If that is even how she ended up here. Time has lapsed between her two nightmares.

Another tremor. Time is not what she should be thinking about. Jessie stands up and stretches her hands out. If she walks in a straight line there is a chance she could find something. Hopefully the woods she had come from. She had been in the woods last time. Her instincts tell her that there has to be trees somewhere. At this point she is going to hold onto any signs of logic. Afraid of the consequences of a world where logic doesn't exist. She tries to go west. She is pretty sure that when finding the meadow she had gone east. Picking directions without light is hard. All she has to do was retrace her steps if the first direction doesn't work out. Just like if she were awake.

Somehow the silence and emptiness is worse than being in the woods. Her hands haven't run into anything yet. Like the darkness is some kind of void, never ending. Suddenly a light mist becomes visible. A squeak of joy escapes her lips - the right direction. Jessie has managed to go west after all. Or maybe she has really floated up. It is hard to tell. The dreams seem to form their own sort of twisted logic in the dark. Feeding off her fear. The thought stops her in her tracks. Unable to move. Deep breaths and relax. Ghosts can't hurt you. That's what she has always believed. She isn't going to stop now.

Other objects start to come into focus as she glances around. Bright lights take the form of people. But something is wrong. Off. They are all distorted. Like looking through a fun house mirror. There is some kind of interference between their world and hers. Or maybe this is what they have always looked like. Taking the form of the dead to trick her into a false sense of security. The reason why she couldn't find anyone with powers quite like hers. They just never had a reason to harm her before. But now something has changed. Reality. In the back of her mind she knows what had changed. The red fog with human emotions. It wants her. Needs her.

These ghosts, no creatures, let out a loud wail. Their form so twisted it now resembles more of a demon from a horror movie than human. Jessie's legs give out. She hits the ground with a hard thump. The whole ground seems to tremble from their cry. This world mourning the coming storm. It is a cry of death. Blind panic sets in. No more. She jumps up and sprints the direction opposite from the screams. From the creatures. At this point she doesn't care if she goes back into the darkness. Somewhere where these new powers of hers couldn't reach her. Or her twisted nightmares.

The mist starts to get thicker. Beginning to blanket her in darkness. At this point Jessie is unsure if the creatures or the dark terrify her more. Both leave her feeling helpless. Confused. She spots a second dimmer light in the distance. She stumbles into the meadow. Back from wherever she had been. It's empty. Once again she's alone. She spots the woods from yesterday. Jessie forces herself back on her feet. Safety isn't far away. Back through the darkness she'd find the sandy path, and her house. She had walked part of this yesterday. Maybe she could even find the boy again, have him help her escape.

She makes a dash for it. Halfway across the meadow she freezes. Unable to move. Fear consumes her as she glances down. Dozens of red hands, unnaturally long, have wrapped themselves around her legs. Coming from the darkness and beginning past the fog. The place the creatures dwell. Waiting to harm her. For their chance to rule. She shakes her head trying to get the voices out. Now isn't the time to panic.

Jessie's feet get ripped out from under her. She claws and digs into the dirt trying to get traction. To stop herself from getting pulled back. Not into the darkness. If she gets pulled back there, she'll be trapped. Evil is winning the battle. More hands spring out of the darkness. Pulling her in inch by inch. Something silver shimmers to her left. She peers over trying to make it out. The shackles and chain the boy had yesterday. She latches on. The screams from the creatures begin to echo out into the meadow. They begin to drown out her own scream as she gets sucked back into the darkness.

20

ZEN LAUNCHES A CHAIR ACROSS THE ROOM, RESISTING THE
urge to toss his phone. The chair shatters against the wall. The black
screen on his phone laughing at him. Since yesterday no one has
answered at Var. The sun has come up on his attempts to reach base.
Something is wrong at home base. The elders never leave phones
unattended. They hate surprises more than anything else. And, boy,
does he have one hell of a surprise to report. His experiment has proven
two things. First, is that the gate is indeed partially open. The second,
and more important discovery, is that there is an Astro close by. Really
close. While in the Abyss, the chain had reacted to an Astro. He has
never seen the chain glow such a bright blue before. The chain couldn't
travel very far into the Abyss. It is less than twenty feet long and part of
that would have been lost reaching the gate. The Astro had to be near
the gate - the Solace gate. He had panicked at the reaction and tried to
pull the chain back through. It had felt like he was pulling a person.
There had been a ton of resistance, like tug of war. However when the
chain returned through the seal it had been alone, and no longer
glowing blue.

Without any response or orders from the elders, Zen is unsure what
to do. He can't seal the gate on his own even if he wanted to. For now
the town is safe. But that won't last long with an Astro playing in the

Abyss. He isn't even sure if the Astro can get out of the Abyss. He remembers hearing stories of Astros getting stuck in the lower levels of the Abyss because they couldn't control their powers. Whether it is true or a myth told to scare the young recruits he can't remember. What he does know is that if the power of an Astro is consumed by one of the more powerful creatures, the battle is already over. The creatures would easily be able to blast the Solace gate wide open.

The only lead he had on the Astro's location is the other house outside of town. It was on the other side of Solace from him. Zen recalls that it had been sold off a few weeks ago. The laws of the Death Walkers state that he should leave the house and the Astro alone, instead focusing on the safety of the town. But he can't. This could be another Heinzer event being created. Or worse an Astro could be in jeopardy. Scared and alone. Just like she had been all those years ago. Helpless.

He shakes his head. He isn't going back to his childhood. He has to focus on the here and now. One wrong move at this point would doom him and the town. Regretting the past would get him nowhere. Besides he had made sure it couldn't happen again. After sealing her memories and her powers, Var had sent her into hiding. Turning her into a normal human who just also happens to carry Astro blood. Oftentimes as the bloodlines get weaker the powers disappear so she shouldn't have ever caught anyone's attention.

Zen scoops up his keys and runs out the doors. He ignores the small imp like creatures hanging around the house. It seems like the seal is changing again. Or another gate really has opened up nearby. He hesitates for a moment - should he send them back through the gate or just ignore them? He debates for a few minutes while they stare at him. Decisions. At this point he could better spend his energy. If all he does is fight off the creatures he will never find the source. But what are they looking for? Sliding into the corvette, he decides to check out the old house. See what kind of family has moved in. It has always been easy for him to spot an Astro on sight. If it proves to be a dead end, he'll search the town again. He isn't going to let Tyr win.

21

JESSIE MANAGES TO RETURN HOME WITHOUT INCIDENT AT school today. After the locker room she it was hard to want to leave the house again. At this rate, she is going to have a heart attack before she understands what is going on. Something about the nightmares is definitely real. The bruises she could have passed off as tossing and turning in her sleep. Doubtful, but it helps her sanity. But now the hands had been in her reality. Pushing over lockers. Plus after the last dream, her clothes had been dirty. And dirt had been trapped under her fingernails. Like she had been dragged somewhere. Something evil is lurking in the woods. Calling to her, waiting. Bringing her to it.

She shivers as she catches a glimpse of the couch. The red cloth matches those hands. She picks up an old sheet up from the floor and tosses it over the couch. For a while she doesn't want to see anything red. Maybe for the rest of her life. It doesn't matter anymore if people think she is crazy. Jessie isn't sure of her own sanity at this point. There is only so much she can blame on her powers. Besides, pretending it is all a hallucination is more comforting than the reality of it being real.

She makes a dash for the closet. To save her sanity she has to go back in the woods. Tearing through the shelves she searches for a flashlight, not wanting to waste time going into town. She finds a bulky flashlight.

Not what she had planned on buying but it should be able to cut through the darkness. Something is lurking out there, and it is coming this way. Maybe if she finds it, whatever it is, she could what? Challenge the thing? Her desire to go after this thing is almost as insane as treating the dreams as real. Her sanity is under attack in more ways than one. But this is the first time she felt that the ghosts could harm her. If they really are ghosts. The way they look in dreams, she questions what she knows about the ghosts. They hadn't been quite human in the dream. She has a sinking feeling that what she saw last night is the truth. Is this her natural power going out of control? Or is something seriously wrong with Solace? Her gut tells her finding those answers is important to her survival.

Deep breaths. She has to focus on one problem at a time. Otherwise she'd have a panic attack before reaching outside. Jessie flings open the back door. These nightmares are not going to control her. And that is that. Once again, she'd go out there proving reality is different from her dreams. It is the isolation driving her crazy. She has never believed in boogeymen and goblins and has no intention of starting now. Especially not because of some stupid dreams. She strides toward the edge of the woods. Building up her courage with each step. Grounding herself in this reality the closer she got.

Nearing the path she entered on a few days ago, her blood runs cold. The courage she had moments ago flees. Drag marks lead into the woods. Like someone or something has been pulled in. Like her. But she had been pulled much further in. Her struggle started in the meadow. So what has made this? What is she going to find going into the woods? For a split second she questions the safety of this plan. The house is so safe. She wipes her hands on her jeans trying to wipe off the sweat. The last thing she needs is to drop the flashlight before she even gets into the woods. This is her chance. The woods won't get much brighter than when the sun is straight up. If it looks too dangerous she could turn around and run, then call her uncle. Or just hop onto a train, and put as much distance between her and Solace as possible. Commit herself for once.

She takes a big step. Jessie is in the woods. She's crossed the line. Determined to recapture her sanity. There is no turning back.

Looking down, she notices the drag marks continue. They go deeper into the woods. And head east, the direction she plans on going. Something had set out to meet her last night. Whatever it is she hopes not to meet it. She can't help but follow the path the drag marks carved into the ground. Like it is beckoning her. Taunting her. She ignores a voice screaming at her to turn around. This is something she has to do, for better or worse. She forces herself to keep going at a brisk pace. If she slows down she is afraid she might turn around and flee. It doesn't take long to reach the darkness. It is a bit foggy as well. She turns on the flashlight before entering the darkness. This time the flashlight is able to make some difference. She can at least see her feet and the drag path. Not much else though. But it is enough to keep her going forward. To not turn around and flee.

It seems like hours before Jessie stumbles out of the darkness. Still following the pre-made path. In front of her is the empty meadow. No ghosts and no boy. A sigh escapes her lips as she determines no red hands either. See? Her mind had been playing tricks on her. Just stand in the middle and reclaim her sanity. She feels silly for letting her powers control her so much. Maybe Sarah's death has affected her more than she originally thought.

Reaching the center, a feeling of dread washes over her. The feeling of victory disappearing. Claw marks begin where the drag marks end. She follows them with her eyes. The location from her nightmares actually exists to some extent. She stares into the brush. The place the claw marks lead. Where she had stumbled out of and was drug back in. Her feet have walked over to the brush before her mind realizes what they're doing. The drag marks pick up with the claw marks. Beckoning her to go back into the darkness. To climb into the brush, like a horrible dare. The hair on the back of her neck stands up. This is suicidal. Why had she thought this a good idea? She pivots around and takes off. This time she follows the path out at a sprint. In less than ten minutes she reaches the edge of the woods. Her home is in sight. The one safe place.

With the house in view Jessie comes to a dead stop. Hovering around near the back porch is the boy. The green-eyed savior. Hanging around his neck is a chain. The same chain she had latched onto in the last nightmare. The carvings on the shackles even match. Though now that she is awake it seems more like a cuff than shackle. What is going on? What kind of rabbit hole has she fallen into? Now she knows how Alice felt in Wonderland. This shouldn't be possible. Her powers allow her to see ghosts. Creatures. Not predict the future. Right? She clamps her mouth shut to keep the scream from escaping her lips when he looks her way.

22

The sun is beginning to set. Zen turns off the engine and coasts into the driveway. The "For Sale" sign is gone but the house is dark. He slides out of the car, adjusting the bracelet. He peers through one of the porch windows. The house is being lived in. There are still boxes in what appears to be the living room. They haven't been here for long. The arrival of these people could match up to the seal and the creatures' actions the past few days. He'll have to check to see when the house sold.

Zen circles to the back of the house. Whoever it is doesn't seem to be home. He needs a visual if he is going to look through the system to see if they carry Astro bloodline. There's no pictures hanging on the walls either. It most likely isn't a family that has moved out here like he had originally thought - he could only ID one bedroom. The house is a lot smaller than the elders described. This is the right road, though. He wonders what happened to the original house. At least this should make it easier to identify a person carrying the Astro blood. He probably only needs to find one or two people at most.

Something is crashing through the woods and approaching the house. Zen glares at the tree line. More creatures? Could there really be a second gate here? He blinks. A short person stumbles out of the woods. How had they made so much noise? It's a girl. She really couldn't be more than five feet tall. Her brown hair flies in the wind. Something about her seems very familiar. Images of his past flash before him. Zen rubs his forehead trying to fight off the headache. He remembers there is someone important to him, someone who he had put into hiding years ago. The world starts to spin around him and his vision blurs. He needs to get out of here.

As she starts to approach him he can sense the Astro blood. Everything comes into focus. It all comes into focus. Tyr's desire to use Astros to take down the seals. The recreation of his past. Where this bracelet came from. The horror of the situation makes Zen's stomach turn. It's her. Jessie. How much does she remember? He tries to slow down his breathing as Jessie approaches. Being calm is his strong point. If he starts babbling to her things would only spiral more out of control. He has to regain some kind of normalcy in this situation. No more following other people's plans. From now on he will be calling the shots.

If she really has been tricked here by Tyr, and this isn't the worst coincidence in history; that means her powers have returned to some extent, the seal on her own powers broken. How else could they have found her? He doesn't remember any betrayals from Var or anyone hacking their database. Zen feels himself tensing up, his hand locked into a ball. He shouldn't think about her anymore. That is a past life. Many identities ago. He's forgotten about it. Has to forget.

"You're the boy from my dream."

"Huh?" her voice rips Zen out of his thoughts.

"My first dream. You were attacked by ghosts in the meadow back there. Where the red hands came from. Then there was another dream. Your chain was there. It pulled me out of the dream and away from the red hands. Away from it. The evil. Why are you in my dreams? What's happening?" Jessie looks like she's going to cry.

"Zen. This is my first time seeing you. Maybe you saw me in your dreams because you caught sight of me in Solace. It's cold out here. I think it's best for you to go in and rest."

Zen ignores her protest as he shoos her inside. That is the worst stammered excuse in history. He just doesn't want to think about her. Or what her powers as an Astro returning means. For everything. He tries to remember the reports about her powers and can't. With her dream in mind, outside isn't a safe place for her. Neither is sleeping apparently. One problem at a time. He had not been attacked in these woods. This is his first time here. Could she be one of the few Astros that can see the future? The idea is terrifying. It would explain the creatures' strong desire to hunt her down. It would be like a moth's attraction to a flame.

Focus. He needs to gain control and figure out what to do. First he needs to follow those tracks into the woods to see what he's dealing with. He can deal with her powers later. If a lower level creature is here, Zen needs to know. If they are able to get here without going through Solace it means another gate has formed. Or at least a tear between the two realms. Hopefully he finds nothing. Without any kind of seal the more powerful creatures could easily escape from the Abyss. One problem at a time. He needs to focus on this world first. See what is actually there. Then he can worry about her slipping into the Abyss when she falls asleep and her dreams. He has to protect her and the city at the same time.

Halfway down the path the drag marks go into a dark bank of trees. The light mist starts to turn into fog. As Zen starts to walk through the fog, fear begins to set in. What if he has to choose between Solace and Jessie? If there is no option between saving her and saving Solace? Does he have the strength to abandon her?

23

THE SUN SET A WHILE AGO. JESSIE HAD BEEN UNABLE TO convince Zen to stay with her. After finding out he's real she's afraid to be left alone. At any moment she expects more things from her dreams to appear on her doorstep. It is the first time she has cried so desperately for someone not to leave her alone. Her entire belief system has been turned upside down in the woods. It is hard to tell which one of them had been more surprised by the encounter. It feels like pulling teeth trying to get him to talk to her. She wonders if he is experiencing the same type of dreams she is. How else has he not found her crazy as she spilled about the last couple days? Unless he knows what is going on. Could he be part of what her nightmare is trying to warn her about? She is going to stay as far away from the woods as possible. No reason to ask for trouble. Besides, right now she isn't able to accept that any part of her dreams are real. It's like her dreams are an alternate reality of some kind. Now she has to debate their meaning if she wants to be able to protect herself from the danger of that red fog creature. Even with her powers, that can't be normal behavior.

Though Jessie does wonder where Zen came from. Someone with those looks and as tall as he is would have caught some attention in Solace. The town has the whole insider-outsider thing going on. They whisper about her to her face. No way they wouldn't whisper about him. She has not seen him in town, she is sure of it. But then how is she able to dream about him? And what the hell is he doing at her house? He is scoping out her home, looking for something. This whole situation is a mess. She is no longer sure of what is reality and what is a dream. Everything seems real. And no one is around to ground her in reality.

For the first time in a long time she feels agitated about not being able to remember her early childhood. Even the physical evidence seems to have been erased. Like she is never meant to know. Those lost memories must hold the key to her questions and his identity. Her gut feelings have never been wrong before. The feeling of being hunted just won't go away. If he is in both realities than there is some truth into what is going on. The whole process is draining, sucking the last of her energy away. If feels more like years since she has arrived in Solace. Not the week it's truly been.

The back door is still unlocked. Originally Jessie had left it open in hopes that Zen would have changed his mind and returned right away. That has not happened. He doesn't seem to sense the danger that she does, or he doesn't care. She isn't sure which bothers her more. He just strides right in the woods. She doesn't want to become part of his normal if this is it. She guesses he is heading to the meadow. It has played an important part in her dream twice. Twice she has had a connection to him there. The only emotion he shows is a slight frown at the drag marks. He'd make a great poker player.

Part of her thinks she should go in after him. Or at least stand near the edge and holler in. See if she can get a response. Zen has been in the woods for hours. But the fear paralyzes her from acting on the impulse. She knows he is still in there. The old corvette he arrived in is still in the driveway. So instead she has kept herself busy. Not letting herself think about the world outside her house. Creating her own reality that exists within these four walls.

Jessie found a bunch of her diaries buried in the book boxes her mom sent. A couple look like they start around the time her memories had kicked back in. If nothing else maybe she has had dreams like this before. Maybe Zen would be mentioned in one of them, or at least someone like him. There's no way her memories can really be behind a brick wall. Something like that would signal an accident, and she hasn't had one. That she is sure of. Sarah had helped her look at old hospital records. Her parents had continued to evade any questions about everything. They don't even have the decency to answer the phone. So the diaries are a last shot at some answers. Doing the investigating on her own is bittersweet. This is something Sarah had loved to do. Had started to do for her. Bringing over stacks of information to sort through on the kitchen table. Letting Jessie focus on controlling her powers and having a normal life. But now the table is empty, and quiet. Leaving her to do both parts of the investigation. She can't help but sigh as she pulls the first book out. Flipping it open to the first page, she fights a yawn. This is going to be a long night.

24

ZEN CRASHES OUT OF THE FOG INTO THE MEADOW. FINALLY
there's light. For a while he was worried he had gotten lost in the fog. It
feels like he had wandered in circles for hours. He can feel the magic
leaking from the Abyss. Soaking into his skin. Calling to him. A rift
between the two realms must be close. If Jessie's dreams agre any
indication the rift is somewhere near the meadow. Maybe he should
have listened to more of her dream.

This new rift will not have a seal. It could be like looking for a needle
in the haystack. He is so rattled by Jessie's appearance that he didn't
think the situation through properly. This is what the Psyren wants -- to
put him in an impossible situation. He plops in the meadow, needing to
calm down. If he keeps at this frantic pace he's guaranteed to screw
this up.

What does the code state he should do? Zen knows the code he is
sworn to uphold. It requires him to shed his emotions and protect the
town, the humans. Jessie's safety is supposed to be secondary. Pieces of
his past bombard him. Betrayal. An old worn down church, with
chipped stain glassed windows. A red giant crashing down on him.

Zen pulls himself out of his thoughts, fidgeting with the bracelet.
His breathing shallow. He jumps up ready to move on, to forget. So far
there are no signs of any creatures. Are they hiding in the shadows

again? Looking around, nothing seems out of place. There's also been no fuzzy, out of focus, areas indicating the rift to the Abyss. Only the fog. But something doesn't feel right. Off. The hairs on his arms stick up. A sinking feeling is forming in his stomach. He pulls out his phone, checking the time. Not wanting too be gone for to long. Zen's breath catches in his throat. Not possible. There's no way he's been here for four hours.

A scream pierces the silence. Jessie? Zen whips around expecting her to be there. Nothing. Where did it come from? He notices a red fog creeping around his feet. It's here. He spins back around chasing the fog back, looking for the source. Where it begins will be a rift. It has to be closer than rushing to the cemetery where the other entrance into the Abyss is.

A soft shimmer to his left. Zen glances over and sees the fog swirling around it. It reminds him of some kind of animal den. It's not very big. There are claw marks leading into the den. This is it but can he really fit into the rift? Another scream. He grits his teeth and dives towards the den. Pressure builds on his chest as he tries to pull himself through the rift. He digs his fingers into the cold dirt walls of the den and pulls, trying to squeeze through.

25

Fox strolls up to the cemetery. He manages to not get carried off by any of the drunken groups. This morning he is able to scout undisturbed. So far he hasn't noticed one person from Var. It almost seems too easy. Like some unseen force is guiding him to his destination unnoticed. Like the fog in Solace. Maybe the creatures in the Abyss want this. Want another Heinzer event to redeem themselves. They were so close to ruling both realms. But that woman, the band of 'heroes', somehow turned the tables. A group of five pushing back the creatures and completely sealing off the Abyss. Most cities have rebuilt. It seems like each city rebuilt makes the memory disappear. Like the creatures were never here. The only permanent damage done to his people, bloodlines linked to the Abyss almost wiped out. People burned in fear. Humans' cruelty is much worse than the creatures'. That's why they need to be reminded, and taught a lesson for their insolence.

A car horn pulls Fox out of his thoughts. He can't believe someone is actually trying to drive when people are packed like sardines in the street. Most appear to be here for the beer. It is more a mockery of the occult than a celebration of it. But he's come to expect that. To actually celebrate it, they would have to go into the darkness. Humans seem to not like the reminder that their existence is fragile. Fueled by the alcohol and youth they believe they are immortal. At least there are plenty of them around. It makes it easier to move around unnoticed. Plus with this many occult going people there should be someone with a link to the Astro bloodline. These type of celebrations tend to attract those type of people. If it doesn't then the board will just have to be patient as seal finishes breaking down on its own.

The green light glows lighting up the cemetery. It seems to have grown from this morning. Calling to him to hurry up. No one but him can see it, or the creatures. It is part of the reason it is so exhilarating to think about letting them out. The dirty humans won't know what hit them. Of course they'd have all kinds of theories as to what is happening. Denying the supernatural. Cowering in fear of the darkness. Eventually running out of places to hide. The downside is that the once the more powerful creatures from the lower levels of the Abyss would be visible when they start coming out of the gate. Undeniable. Easier to hide from. But that's also when Tyr would be there to sweep in and take over. Destroying Var forever. Leaving only the superior organization to care for the Abyss. Maybe years later they might even try to recreate the Death Walker race. Assuming anyone ever figures out the mystery of how Death Walkers were originally created.

Laughter escapes his lips as he approaches the edge of the seal. This has been too easy. Not one Death Walker has been around to even challenge him. Maybe the Var outpost near here has been abandoned like so many other outposts. After all, the Heinzer event had almost annihilated the Death Walkers. The one group that could fight the creatures hardly exists any more. What the creatures haven't destroyed, the humans have. Another hundred bloodlines wiped out due to human justice. The irony has been bittersweet. They had laid down their life to save the humans only to be killed by the people they had saved. They are treated as more evil than the creatures themselves. It's why he hates the blood in his own veins and wanted to destroy it all. The images of his sister burning flashes in front of his eyes.

For a moment Fox is saddened by the lack of challenge these towns have been. He hoped for one good battle, but there is still time for that. Maybe he can even go back to Solace in time for Zen's destruction. Introduce himself to the last pure blood Death Walkers after all. It is hard to believe that with all Zen has seen he still supports Var's stance on protecting the humans. Yet he protects an Astro from the humans. His hypocrisy is astounding. Fox can never understand why the Death Walkers continue to protect the very people hell bent on destroying them. They'll learn the error of their ways soon enough. The revolution will never be stopped. He is proof of this.

Fox lifts his hand towards the seal. The green glow is soothing as it starts to swell and grow. Maybe he'll pop the seal on his own. A frown crosses his face as the ground trembles. That hadn't been something he had been warned about. Maybe the Death Walkers have set a trap after all. He tries to stop but can't move his hand. It is like something else is controlling his magic. And him. What is going on? He glances around. No one is nearby. Fox tries to scream. His mouth won't open. Panic starts to take over. He tumbles forward as something pulls his body towards the gate. Impossible. He's being pulled through the seal. That isn't something a Psyren is able to do. Is this the true power of the creatures of the Abyss? Have the seals been unnecessary all along? Fox tries to grab onto a tombstone as he is pulled into the gate. A scream pierces the night sky as the gate closes, trapping Fox inside.

26

Jessie is standing outside of her house. Something is off. There's not only been a time lapse but a change in location. This dream is somehow different. More real. And more dangerous. She feels the change as the hair on the back of her neck stands up. The air feels charged. Not in a good way. But which way to go? The voices battle in her head. House? Woods? And where is Zen? Shouldn't he be around here? It's hard for her to decide where to go. Both choices feel dangerous. A third choice her mind can't figure out. She needs to move.

Her eyes keep being drawn towards the woods. Movement. Something large is in the woods behind her. The creatures are coming. She starts to stumble backwards. She cuts her hand on the rock as she loses her balances. The porch isn't far away. She needs to run for it. Her house has always been the end goal. Out of the red creatures' way. The snapping of branches echoes through the woods towards her. Advancing towards the house. Surrounding her. Paralyzing her. She tries to call out but her voice won't come out, catching in her throat. She licks her lips and tries again. Nothing.

This part of the dream she's on her own. So think. And move. Jessie jumps up as something comes out of the woods. Hundreds of ghosts, no creatures, flee past her and the house towards the road, heading out of the area. This time they're not moving in slow motion. They're in a dead sprint. Not wanting to be caught by the thing in the woods. Another snapping branch. Closer. She snaps out of it and cries out for Zen. No response. This is the creatures' reality. A reality without Zen. Is he not near the house or has that thing in the woods already gotten him? Both thoughts send chills down her spine. She cries out again. The only response is the snapping of branches. It's near the edge of the woods. Heavy breathing starts to come from the woods. She has to decide what to do. Now.

She dashes for the back porch. The fear winning. She scrambles for the back door, ignoring the creatures that are running past the house. She tries the handle to the back door of the house. She's not surprised that it's unlocked. Just like she left it when she was awake. This thought causes her to hesitate - that means reality is linked with the nightmare. A wrong choice here could harm her, or kill her. Her hands tremble as she tries to wrap them around the door handle. She looks back over her shoulder. A feeling of dread washes over her at the thought of going inside. But the red hands are found in the woods. What could be worse than those red hands? And the darkness? No time to turn back. Jessie flings the door open.

Her scream bounces off the walls. The red fog greets her in the living room, the blood lust pouring from it. She stumbles backwards. She should have gone for the woods. Jessie tries to scramble back onto her feet as she screams for Zen again. Praying for an answer. She has to get out of here. Feet. She has to get back on her feet.

Dozens of red hands shoot out from the fog. They head right for her. Somehow able to see her. To seek her out. She feels the door behind her. Half crawling, half running she stumbles back out onto the porch. Screaming. She feels the red hands wrap around her legs. Terror consumes her. Not again. Not a third time. This time she has to fight. She kicks and screams as the hands drag her back into the house, to the fog. She wraps her hands on the door frame. She has to buy time. Zen is close. She can hear someone running towards the house.

The hands continue to multiply. Piling on top of each other. There seems to be no end to the creatures' power. The hands reach up and start prying her hands off the frame. A blood curdling scream echoes through the house. The creature is winning. It always wins. The hands lift her in the air. Jessie reaches out trying to find something to hold onto. Anything. She slams into the ceiling. Air hisses out of her lips and she hears the sound of something breaking. The hands let go, letting gravity take over. White light flashes in her eyes as she bounces on the floor. More cracking sounds. She tries to scream. Only a whimper escapes her lips. Her energy drains away. She is unable to move. Her willpower gone. The room spins around her as the red hands wrap around her again. She can't survive a second round. Something shimmers behind the fog. She hears a gunshot ring through the house as her world goes black.

27

ZEN CURSES AS HE URGES THE CORVETTE TO CLIMB THE mountain faster. It had been midnight before they both emerged from the Abyss. He listens for Jessie's light breathing in back. Praying that this is the worst of it. She had been a mess by the time he reached her. His return trip from the woods had been slow and painful. This is the second time in less than a week that he had walked right into a trap. Doing exactly what the creatures wanted. Maybe it is time for him to retire. Stop the charade, he's making too many mistakes.

It's obvious now that it is her spiritual body that has been going into the Abyss while she is asleep. Astros don't need the power of the gate to travel into the Abyss. He had known this. That is where the danger has been all along. Why has he been assuming the Astro was using a gate? Hopefully she's too out of it for her powers to pull her back. Zen can't go another round with the creatures. He pulls one hand off the steering wheel to cradle his throbbing ribs. He tries not to think about how many of them broke during his attempt to enter the Abyss. Forcing his way into the Abyss had not been easy on his body. It's becoming hard to hold on the steering wheel as the cuts on his hand stiffen his fingers. He never wants to use brute force to break into the Abyss again.

He's now out of ammo after shooting at the creature. The worst part is it didn't really do anything to it. Annoying it is all he achieved. That is a creature from the lower levels that has made its way up near the gate. Zen will have to find a different way to take that creature on. He can't remember a time that his weapon is so useless. He just prays that it doesn't attack again until he can get some backup.

His vision begins to blur. Zen slams on the breaks trying to gain control. The world spins as he becomes unable to block out the pain. Almost there. He takes long deep breaths trying to push it back. As the world comes back into focus he eases the corvette back on the road. He tosses a glance in the backseat. Her breathing is starting to slow. He needs to get to the hospital.

A glowing sign beckons their safe arrival. He's made it. Just one more corner. Another stab of pain. This is only the second time his powers seem useless. Inferior. He hates it. It's why it had been so easy to walk away after everything ended. He clings to his humanity but hates reminders of it. Zen shakes his head. Now isn't the time for that. He has to get in the hospital doors. After that, find a way to get someone's attention at Var. This time there are not options. Jessie is coming into the organization.

A sigh of relief as the ER doors come into sight. His own nightmare is almost over. The fight in the Abyss tonight seems to stay in the Abyss, which is kind of bittersweet. His other side still wants to go another round with the creature. Zen knows that in his current state his body couldn't handle another round. Besides the more interaction they have with it the bigger the chance that it escapes. He only needs it to stay in the Abyss for a few more days. Surely after all this Var will ship out a Psyren immediately to get the seal repaired. A creature like this could destroy several cities in a few hours.

Zen slams on his breaks almost zooming past the entrance to the emergency room doors. He peels himself out of the corvette. Some nurses notice them. The doors slide open as they rush out. Hopefully he has reached the hospital in time. The nurses are carrying a bunch of supplies with them. When they try to come for him he waves them off, motioning to Jessie. He makes sure they take off with her first. Before they can come out for him he pushes himself off the ground. Zen has enough pride left to walk himself into the hospital. His penance for always making the wrong choices. Solace has become his own type of hell. As he drags himself into the hospital he tries to block out the shimmering red hand prints on the front door.

95

28

JESSIE'S HEAD IS POUNDING. THE WORLD STARTS TO SLOWLY come into focus. What time is it? Hell, what day is it? Where is she? A soft groan escapes her lips. She forces her eyes open despite the bright light. She tries to assess her situation. Piece reality back together. White everything and an IV in her arm. Must be a hospital. No restraints so most likely she isn't in a mental institute. That is a good start. The light becomes overbearing. She loses the fight and her eyes fall shut.

There's a lack of voices. Jessie tries to listen for someone and get some answers. She feels herself nodding off. There is something soothing about the beeping sound from all the machines. Hypnotic. She forces her eyes back open. She needs to at least figure out how beaten up she is before dozing off. Jessie tries to remember what happened. How she ended up here, but everything is fuzzy. She wiggles her fingers. They're numb. Must be on some pretty strong medication, keeping her in a haze.

Someone comes near her door. Faint voices float through the wall. She tries to make out the voices to see if it's about her. Get some kind of clue of what's going on. The voices are unintelligible. Has she been out long enough for her parents to arrive? Or is it just nurses gossiping? She can't even make out the tone of the voices to know. Jessie struggles to remember what happened. What's the last thing she did?

There is the meeting with Zen. The sun setting. Jessie trying to stay up and wait for him to exit the woods. And the diaries. Looking for answers about her powers. But then what? After that it is blank. Had she dozed off? Slipped into another one of her nightmares? But that doesn't explain how she has wound up in a hospital. All she can remember was the color red. And hands.

Jessie tries to sit up and pain runs through her body. Is there some broken pieces? She takes a deep breath as she tries to check out the rest of her body. No casts but a lot of tape around her mid-section. Something with her ribs?

Before the pain knocks her out she glances around the room. In a corner she notices Zen sitting in a chair. Lightly snoring. A lose bandage around his hand, his wounds mostly healed. She must have been out for a while. So where are her parents? Zen looks to be about three sizes too big for the chair, like some stuffed him in it. Even his legs dangled several inches over the foot rest. She hadn't really paid attention to how tall and broad he is. A soft chuckle escapes her lips as she watches him try to shift around in his sleep, causes her to wince.

As she lays back down she wonders what is already mended. Carefully she pulls back the covers to see what's there. There's bruises covering her body and stitches running up her side. And that's just the parts she could see. Part of her wants to yell out. To wake him up. Demand answers. If he is here that means he has an idea of what happened. But he looks so exhausted. And worried. It can wait. Besides she's so tired. Jessie's vision starts to blur. The whir of a machine. Something is filling the IV tube. She tries to fight it off. The thought of sleeping terrifies her. She isn't sure she can survive another dream. Her eyes refuse to stay open. The beeping of the machines gets softer as she feels herself drifting away.

Another dream. Jessie spins around. Nothing red is around. Just a cemetery off in the distance. It feels empty this time. More peaceful, and serene. For the first time ever she finds a cemetery safe. Probably because she is far away from the terrors near her home. A sigh of relief escapes her lips. She is in a more normal dream, or at least a safer one. She checks herself over. No injuries. So her injuries seem to travel only one way. At least she could explore freely. Besides, who knows? Several years could have passed in this dream world. Time and space seem to operate on a different scale here.

As she reaches the entrance to the cemetery she discovers a rickety old gate, one hinge left holding it in place. The sign is falling down and illegible. For a moment her safe feeling is broken by the disrepair of the cemetery. There's something uneasy about such an abandoned cemetery. Surely there are some families that still come out and care for the graves. And where exactly is this cemetery? Could this be in Solace? She couldn't remember seeing one, but she's never gotten past Main Street. So it is possible her dream is of Solace cemetery. With the amount of graves, this place has to be pretty old, probably started when Solace had a much bigger population. The tombstones go on for as far as she can see.

Jessie keeps looking around as she wanders the cemetery. Glancing at the dates and trying to understand why the cemetery could have become so neglected. There's got to be a reason her dreams moved to a cemetery. Is something trying to show her something or is a creature trying to finish her off? A greenish light in the distance catches Jessie's eye. She starts walking toward it. Watching the tombstones get older and older. As she gets further back the tombstones are all in different stages of decay.

She stops to catch her breath as she nears what she thought is the back of the cemetery. Instead she's come across another gate. It's like a cemetery inside of a cemetery. She looks around for a sign. Wondering if someone built a new cemetery around this older one, or some reason why this area is sectioned of. There's no other signs or statutes making it seem more important. So why the isolation? She's never seen a cemetery do something like this before. The tombstones inside are almost completely hidden, overtaken by nature. It's been a long time since someone was buried in this section. Jessie eases the gate open, afraid of it falling off. Once it's open enough she slides through, moving forward. The green aura acting as a strange sort of beacon.

She starts to feel uneasy about the lack of life. There's not even the distant chirping of crickets. The crinkling of the leaves seem to echo around her as she walks. She wonders how far the crunching sound will carry. Can the creatures hear it? Will the red hands finally pop out of the ground as she walks by? Jessie shakes her head trying to push out the thoughts. No more horror movies for her for a while.

Jessie stops and bends down to get a better look at one of the tombstones. Something seems different about them. She uses her sleeve to push away the brush to get a better look. This tombstone is not written in English. Weird. Maybe it's just this one. As she goes around to different tombstones she finds the strange language on all of them.

A chill runs down her spine. She feels the presence of the creature. Jessie spins around expecting to see it. She's still alone. Looking around she realizes it's coming from the graves. Images of zombies flash in front of her. Jessie jumps to her feet. She makes a dash for the final gate, wanting to put some distance between her and the graves.

The final gate is in better shape than the rest of the cemetery. It glides open. The green glowing dome seems to be drawing Jessie in. As her desire grows to touch it, her hand moves towards it on its own. Wanting to touch it. Understand it. The green light seems to dim, reacting to her. The green light is replaced by a yellow bubble. It traps the green bubble inside it.

Beyond the green glow Jessie can make out the hazy shape of a gate. She doesn't like the vibe the gate is giving off. Jessie takes a few steps back. As she does, a woman starts to take shape in the center of the yellow bubble. The woman just sits on one of the tombstones, oblivious to the world around her. Like she is waiting for someone or something. A tired guard. But something seems off about the woman. She's different from the creatures but also similar. Jessie wants to reach out to her, attracted to her in much the same way as the green bubble earlier.

Jessie's awe struck by the woman's long silver hair that seems to never end. And her eyes - they're yellow. Almost matching the color of the moon. Jessie's gut is telling her the woman isn't entirely human. Safe but not human. And someone familiar. Important to Jessie somehow. She finds herself approaching the yellow bubble again. Wanting to reach out to the woman. She realizes the woman is trying to talk. Why isn't the sound reaching her? Jessie tries to walk through the barrier but it knocks her back. Not letting her inside. Jessie stares at the woman. She rubs her eyes and looks again. The woman behind the barrier is becoming transparent. Wait. She still hasn't figured out the message yet. She strains her eyes. Watching her lips. As the woman keeps trying to tell her something she disappears. Message unheard. Leaving only the yellow barrier that traps the growing green light.

29

<hr>

It's been two weeks since he brought Jessie to the hospital. It seems like an eternity. Ruffling sheets. Zen snaps back to reality. Uncurling in the chair he notices Jessie is up. How long has it been since she last opened her eyes? The mental battle of the past couple weeks had been worse than the physical beatings he took before. Since arriving, all the activity seems to have stopped. The last sign coming from any creatures had been when entering the hospital. Somehow it seems like they can't track her here. But why wouldn't they be able to find her? There doesn't seem to be anything special about the hospital. Whatever the reason, the situation is fine by him. Everything still hurts. He doesn't want to think how painful the encounter would have been if he didn't possess creature blood, most of his wounds healed in a couple days.

He strolls over to her bed. Jessie shifts around making room for him on the edge of the bed. Thank god she can move. For a while he has been afraid she'd be paralyzed. Unsure what all had been broken in the battle with that red fog like creature. He stares at her unsure of what to stay. How can he word everything that happened without sounding crazy? This is why he avoids people. Conversations are so awkward. Trying to explain the Abyss isn't easy. It's also time consuming. He jumps when her hand falls onto his. Her gentle smile melts away his unease.

"I had another dream. This one was different though."

"How was it different? Did anything come after you?"

"No. At least not that I could see. I was in a cemetery. There was green aura near the back. But it was contained in another bubble. In the center of the bubble was a woman. She had silver hair and eyes the color of the moon. Before she disappeared it seemed like she was trying to tell me something."

"You saw the seal. The green aura was sealing a gate into the Abyss. It's where the things that attacked you live. A realm attached to this one. As for the woman, I've never met her. I'll look into it. So try to get some sleep. You're safe here."

It isn't hard to convince her. Zen only has to wait for a few minutes before she dozes back off. Seems like the pain meds are still doing their job. But something about the dream bothers him. The cemetery she saw is most likely the one in Solace. But who is the woman? There is no one that fit that description in either organization. Could it be some creature just picking an appearance at random? But it seems to be protecting the gate. He can't think of any creature that would want to protect the seal. But that only leaves a Psyren reaching out to her. But it should be impossible that a Psyren is in the Abyss. Var is always saying that the Psyren can't survive in the Abyss. That the air inside the Abyss became toxic shortly after the Heinzer event. This is definitely a strange new development, but what hasn't been in Solace.

Zen walks over to the window trying to work out what Jessie could have seen. The power the woman displayed would have taken a lot of strength. There couldn't be too many Psyren that could have done it. Like the Death Walkers, pure blooded Psyren are also almost wiped out. For some reason the power originally given to the original followers hasn't passed down to their children.

This isn't something he will be able to figure out on his own. Not with his broken memories. As long as this woman doesn't pose a threat it could go on the back burner until he gets some backup. Zen's got enough to worry about right now. Thankfully he finally is able to get ahold of someone back at Var. The elders have a hard time swallowing the news of what all went down the past few weeks. His new orders are to become Jessie's body guard and that's it. They don't believe that this is going to be the end of it. The fact that she was lead here by Tyr, rubbed the elders the wrong way. Their egos had probably been knocked down a couple notches knowing someone hacked into their system.

Part of Zen regrets that he still can't go after the person who started this mess. The idea of beating the Psyren into a pulp is really appealing after everything that has happened for a couple reasons. One is because he knows there is no way he'd trust anyone else to protect Jessie. There's no way that one person can take on that creature if it decides to return. The second is the elders are sending another Death Walker to help protect Jessie and he doesn't like working with others. Not to mention it's a greater risk of getting caught with his messed up memory.

At lease he is getting out of explaining to Jessie how the Astro powers work. That is going to be done by the other Death Walker they are sending out. Hopefully he will be able to sit in on some of the lessons to help piece his own memory back together.

The elders are finally getting around to sending a Psyren to reseal the gate into the Abyss, along with the rift he had found in the meadow. Solace being so close to destruction seems to have changed their tune a bit. If all goes well the Psyren will only have to be here a couple days and no one in Solace will be any wiser. While the Psyren will leave after their work is done it's not so clear for Jessie and himself. For once the elders are split on the issue. Most want to see what Tyr's next step is before moving Jessie anywhere. That and confirm how they are keeping tabs on her. At least he's regaining some control of the situation.

Fox feels like he's fallen forever. Where did he end up? He wishes he paid more attention to the lessons about the Abyss, but he never thought he'd be here. He knows that there are four levels which humans can travel to. This can't be fourth level since it's not complete darkness. He stays on edge in case he's on the third level. There are horror stories about the kind of creatures who live down here. More animalistic in appearance and action.

A path of trees sits in front of him. Fox stands up and starts following the trees. Glancing back and forth for any danger. He's still not sure why or how he was pulled into the Abyss. Through the tunnel of trees he spots an old house. He glances all around looking for the creatures who would call this place home. All he can see is the trees. He runs his fingers through his hair trying to decide what to do. There's a reason he was brought to this part of the Abyss but he isn't too big on the idea of walking into a house. Too many blind corners. But if he wanders around he's likely to find a creature of some type that didn't bring him here. One that will see him as food. Fox decides to risk the house.

As he nears the house he continues to search for the creature that pulled him here. Without that creature there is no chance of Fox getting out of here. Like the Death Walkers he is dependent on the Astros, or in this case creatures, to be able to come and go from the Abyss. The joys of being in another realm. Though why has he been pulled inside the gate in the first place? As far as he can tell there are no creatures here. Creatures just don't pull people inside the Abyss for the hell of it. There must be a reason he's here and still in one piece.

He tries the door handle. Unlocked. Fox pushes the door open. He cringes at the doors creaking protest at being opened. He spins around, sure all the creatures in the Abyss heard it. The gnarled trees remain silent. Maybe leaning in closer but still leaving him alone. He strolls through the house. Empty. He looks around trying to decide what type of creature would live there. Maybe this is where the Death Walkers came from. It seems odd that the creatures would recreate a village from Earth inside the Abyss. Almost like they were domesticated, human in nature. Fox shakes his head. The creatures don't come to Earth just to set up house like a human.

Drawn to a dark room, he peers inside. Still waiting for his host to appear. Something is carved onto the walls. The red mist outside is darkening. Night must be falling in the Abyss, or whatever their equivalent is. There seems to be lights attached to the ceiling. He runs his hand along the wall seeing if there's some kind of switch. Fox takes a deep breath before trying the light switch. He jumps when it flicks on. A blue light flickers on, reminding him of fox fire. That isn't something he saw coming. The creatures have mimicked some kind of electricity. Though he doesn't have time to figure out how it works.

As he searches the room he begins to wonder if this is another trick planned by the creatures. Their own twisted version of hunting their prey. Words like 'her' 'find' 'bring' are scrawled everywhere. He tries to understand who they want. The woman who sealed the gates from the inside? That didn't make any sense. She is already inside the Abyss. No matter how good she is, no one could hide in the Abyss for thirty years without being spotted. So who? He feels something under his feet. He stoops over to pick it up. A broken frame covered in claw marks sits broken inside. Fox carefully pulls the broken glass and cardboard away from the picture. The air here has affected it. He can still make out the image of a little girl with silver blond hair and brown eyes. The name however has yellowed and is no longer legible. This must be who the creatures are after. But who is it?

The room begins to shake. Fox stumbles out of the house before it disappears. The trees begin to fade in the mist. What's happening? The world spins as he gets sucked up. Clinging onto the picture he lands with a thud. Here the mist is more like a thick fog. The creatures on this level are roaming around in their natural form. He reaches out to touch one of the white wisps as it floats by. His hand goes right through.

Fox stands up and starts wandering around. Not wanting to hang around and meet the creature that keeps bouncing him around the Abyss. He notices a green glow penetrating the darkness. Only one thing could make that color here. He's near a seal, and that means there is a gate out of the Abyss nearby. He slides the picture into his pocket. Fox sprints towards the green glow ready to be out of here. A red fog surrounds him, small hands peering out. Is this the thing that dragged him here? Fox freezes. He waits for it to devour him, pulling him back down. But nothing happens. It finds the picture in his pocket and seems happy. Fox swears he can hear it humming. This must be why he had been brought here. This creature wants this girl from the human world. For some reason he has been chosen to retrieve her, and retrieve her he shall. If he makes this creature happy it might return the favor when the two realms are combined once again. The red hands continue to float around Fox as he walks through the gate back to the human world.

WANT TO KNOW WHAT HAPPENS NEXT?

∾

In book two of the Death Walker series their world is turned upside down. Jessie struggles to figure out who she can trust as her powers continue to grow. Zen builds a wall between himself and the world as his creature blood take over. Fox questions his decisions as he struggles to keep the creature under control.

∾

Learn more about Divided Loyalties at annamward.carrd.co

∾

Want to stay up to date on the series?

∾

Check out the main website at ztopianbookgroup.com to join the newsletter.

ABOUT THE AUTHOR

Anna M. Ward lives in the Midwest. Her cat acts as the editor in chief. She prefers writing horror or dystopain stories for the YA and NA genres.